To Sandy, good wishes for the
future, and good luck.

Harold W. Phillips

Another Day the World's Way

H. Wells Phillips

VANTAGE PRESS
New York

FIRST EDITION

Copyright © 2004 by H. Wells Philips

Published by Vantage Press, Inc.
419 Park Ave. South, New York, NY 10016

Manufactured in the United States of America
ISBN: 0-533-14818-9

Library of Congress Catalog Card No.: 2004096266

0 9 8 7 6 5 4 3 2 1

To Joan Walker, whose experiences motivated me
to write this

There are persons; and there are the unrelenting, sometimes rewarding, sometimes humiliating, sometimes vicious intimacies of seconds—yes, very seconds—minutes,
hours, places, actions, and responses that make up their
lives.

When our time is up, we people must not bear malice, but
neither must we forget: we must tell the whole thing, without altering one word . . . ; and then, it will be over and
time to go. That is enough of a job for a whole lifetime.

A Day

I wish she'd post that sheet and get it over with. Think there were a hundred of us instead of just eight. What is so complicated about eight assignments? Three more weeks in this place and it'll be all over, and I can leave for good. And back to Fulton . . . six more months and I can stop giving my time away. Maybe a good deal at Fulton, at least not this place, and the pay would be better.

What's taking her so long? She knows we've got the weekend off. Gave up my lunch, that's not the first time, as if anyone cared, to get those behavior studies finished by three-thirty. I'll be writing those ridiculous things in my sleep from now on.

Well, it's about time . . . here she comes, swinging her arms way out to the sides in that funny way, like her elbows were on broken hinges in a windstorm . . . swinging out of control . . . and her jumpy walk on bowlegs. She's going to fall apart, or explode, before she gets here. Assistant nursing superintendent big deal.

Good to be tall. Let's see, one, two, three, four, Elizabeth Seward. Fulton, WVW Monday. Where does she get that Elizabeth stuff? Two and a half months, she calls me Betty, now it's Elizabeth. What did Cookie get? Six, seven, Susan Koch, occupational. Not so bad.

"Well, Cookie, I had to get it sometime. You'll like occupational."

"The only thing I haven't had. What are you going to do this weekend?"

"I'm getting out of here, that's certain. Why don't you come home with me? You can't get the afternoon train now . . . they've kicked away almost all of today, as it is."

"I'd love it, if it's not any trouble. Don't want to go home, anyway. Better call though."

A Day

I walk to work each morning, certainly different from striding business fashion to some office cubicle. Nothing to stride for here, but would it be different there? Time for sunlight, though, to enjoy . . . even squinting. I must be night people, always squint, at the beginning. What is it? The inception, yes.

There's haggard Mr. Monroe and eyes peering brightly over the bushes at, at what? Lopsided world. Balances himself there, same spot every day: red-faced, and rat's nest hair; wrinkled, out-sized jacket; spattered, zipper-open pants; and scuffed shoes, . . . his rough red hands rigidly at sides. Fingers moving, though, continually, twiddling back and forth, alert swollen antennae probing the air . . .

"Hello, Mr. Monroe. How are you this lovely morning?"

"Fine, fine, fine. Fine. Many bushes to finish today. Have you seen my bushes?"

"Yes, I have. Do finish them. We hope you will."

Must keep walking. Have heard about the bushes, or bush. At least, they've given him a sense of usefulness. Maybe he saved it himself. Fifteen years . . . and he lives on and on. Funny about sunlight here, for these people, like him, first thing it is day's end in the morning and all over in the beginning. Is it really like that? Do they look forward to the sunshine? Of course.

Front gate there. If I walked in for the first time, all this would seem like an old campus . . . even with the fence. Forget the fence. Some stand there all day, looking out. Freedom stops there. They can feel it. They know it.

Even in sunlight, though, look at it, and see, too. One new building for fifteen hundred women, not bad. The rest? Like looking for the thousandth time, but really the first, at the drugstore near home. Really different. Look. There. And at that one. And that one. Barren. No architectural grace, and brick monotony; nothing but red brick. Even the windows, measure them with my thumbnail, same thumbnail row after row, doesn't change. Father used to say believe in it if you do it, or don't do it. He'd say that about these buildings, I know. He'd say whoever built them had no principles. Two and three stories of no principles.

I wonder if he went through all this, medicine, hydros, sedatives. Probably did. I'm sure of it. Occupational, recreational, must have. But no difference now.

And now more two stories of red brick, and rows of narrow windows covered with wire mesh. They're not kidding when they say locked ward, with only one way out, and not through the door. If a fire, what? Steps foot-worn stone and two park benches either side of the door.

For what?

Look . . . it stands abruptly like some poor joke out of the fresh grass and dew and full-bloomed sycamores. Spirited greeting of a gentle spring wind.

Yes, a sorry affair, standing there, forgotten, decayed, and weather-beaten; drain pipes dead long ago from corrosion; and water-stained red brick. No paint, sun-scarred wood showing bare and gray. What a mess. Surrender. Seriously ill building for seriously ill, but why should it be this way?

Same inside, I suppose.

Yes.

4

It is.

Some lobby: one table and two chairs. At least the floor is clean, almost gray from bleaching. Let me see, two doors closed, one slightly open. Must be the ward supervisor. Yes. Fixing her cap, sees me in her mirror. Taking her time to turn around.

"Are you Miss Fenwick?"

Probably is. R.N. pin on her uniform.

"That's correct. Your name, please."

"Here is my assignment card." Younger than I expected, maybe thirty-five, brunette, good skin, and attractive, good figure, too. Certainly deliberate the way you take the card. Sit down. Haven't even looked at the card, keep looking at your desk.

"Your name?"

What's the matter with you, it's right on the card. Why don't you look at it?

"Betty Seward, Fulton Hospital."

"I see. How did you know my name?"

Nice of you to look up.

"Why . . . why, I guess I asked one of my classmates who had been here before."

"Which one?"

"I really don't remember." I can play, too. "Why do you ask?"

"What did she say?"

Wouldn't hurt to risk a smile, you know.

"She said that your name was Miss Fenwick."

Well, isn't that nice—a name plate on polished wood, "KATHERINE FENWICK." First one I've seen around here. Should have said I saw your name here. No answer, eh? Now what're you doing?

"These are your keys, Miss Seward. You will note that all doors leading to the patients' areas are locked, and they

5

are kept locked. The necessity for this is obvious, I think. Now over here, . . . you will note particularly that this door is locked. This leads to the day room. Patients occasionally try to get in here to talk to me or annoy me in some way. This, naturally, would never do. So be sure that when you come in here, lock the door behind you."

"You mean this leads directly to the day room?"

"No, there is a hallway. You'll see it. But the day room is only a few feet away."

"I see."

Oh, oh, more papers.

"Now, then, here is a short outline of your instructions. It includes a description of the ward, for orientation purposes, instructions for writing behavior studies, nursing studies, and so forth, which is homework. You can't do these here. You will also see there a brief discussion of the phenobarbital therapy . . ."

It's long enough, take me two hours just to read it. Still using.

". . . please learn your responsibilities thoroughly. Also, familiarize yourself with hydro-therapy treatments as applied here . . ."

What do you mean, 'as applied here'? Probably mean threatments, not treatments.

". . . if you have questions from time to time, I'm here for that purpose. In that filing cabinet you'll find the charts. The attendants do not have access to them, but you will, since you are in training. You'll need the information there for your studies. So feel welcome to come into the office. Now, let me show you around. Oh, one more thing . . ."

You don't have to show me how to unlock and lock a door.

"Miss Seward, I am familiar with your hospital, and I

know the kind it is . . . an expensive, well-staffed institution for those who can pay the price . . ."

You haven't heard of hospitalization insurance.

". . . the trouble with you girls is that you come here with preconceived ideas about average hospital care. This place, you should know by now, is quite different from a hospital—"

"I know that." Medicine's been table talk at home since I was hem high.

"Nevertheless, this place, particularly this ward, is not set up principally for the patients' comfort. We try to be functional and expedient. You're going to see some unpleasant things, I suppose . . ."

I've been here over two months, and I've already seen enough unpleasant things to last me until I die.

". . . do not, under any circumstances, let sentiment interfere. Remember that some of these women . . . there are nearly 150 altogether . . . are dangerous potential killers. Is that clear? I tell you this, as I tell each new student, only for your own good."

"Yes, I understand."

"You are older than the other girls in your class?"

"Not so much."

"What I mean is, you are two or three years older?"

Thanks for explaining.

"Yes, I was in pre-med until my father died."

"Oh, I see. Well, fine. Then let me take you around. After that, you will alternate your duty between sedative therapy and the tub room."

"How many other students are there here?"

"Oh, yes. The number will vary, but you should have at least three or four working with you. There are usually eight altogether on the wards at one time. Days only."

"Who else works here?"

7

"The ward is regularly staffed with five or six attendants, on days."

"I suppose MDs make regular rounds every day?"

"No—"

No? What do you mean, 'no'? They must.

". . . there's no necessity for it. There's one assigned
here for EST and can be called in for an emergency."

"I see." That's incredible. They could have an emergency around here every two minutes, I'll bet, but no, 'he
can be called.' "Well, I guess we can go."

Step into the hallway. Lock the door. Must remember
that. This place couldn't be plainer and darker. Old
wooden floors, poor, poor lighting. One door at the end,
each end.

"Will you wait here, Betty?"

Now where are you going? Another attendant. Glum.
Plain, no, homely, no, ordinary. All-American guard. Look
at those legs, that torso, that stride.

"Miss Barnes will show you upstairs. Nancy, this is
Betty Seward."

"Hi, Betty."

Smile at least.

"Hello."

"I'll be in my office."

Walk away again. What do you mean, in your office?
Shut, click.

"I thought she said she was going to show me around?"

"Honey, she always says that, . . . but then she asks one
of us to do it. C'mon . . . I'll take you upstairs."

Steep, old worn stairs, creaking every step. Should at
least be a light somewhere. Hardly see where I'm going in
broad daylight. What a firetrap this is. So this is what they
call a dormitory . . . just a bunch of rooms, like wash on a

8

line. Large, all right, but no cross-ventilation. Barren, dark, like everywhere else in the building.

Bare floors, well-scrubbed, but cold looking. Beds no more than a foot apart. . . . Let's see, . . . one, two sheets, pillow, hard mattress. Stretcher in the corner against the wall. Several mattresses on the floor. Can hardly walk without stepping on one.

"What about all these mattresses? Have to crowd so many in like this?"

"Got to put them someplace, you know. Get just so many beds in a room. Kind of bad, but that's the way it is."

You can shrug your shoulders, but you don't sleep here.

What is that? I'm seeing things. What is *that* by the wall?

"Nancy, what is that? That is the biggest mouse trap I ever saw—no, it's a rat trap, isn't it?"

"That's right."

"You have rats here?"

"I don't have them. They're around."

"Good God, you could break a foot if you tripped into it."

"That's right."

You take it lightly enough.

"Why are the doors locked? Supposing a patient gets sick. Someone would have to let her in—"

"They have to stay downstairs. We don't let them up during the day."

"Oh, are there extra beds downstairs?"

"Are you kidding? If they get sick, they lie on the floor in the day room. We got enough to do without playing nursemaid."

"So these rooms stay empty all day?"

9

"That's right, all day. Say, honey, . . . let me tell you something. What'd you say your name was?"

"Betty."

"Oh, yeah. Well, listen, Betty, you ask too many questions. Don't get me wrong. I don't mind, but a couple of people around here might."

"Oh, yes? But it won't keep me from asking."

"Okay by me. It's your funeral, not mine."

Dark hall again. Look at that walk, arms at side like you were muscle-bound. Fat palms. Should be wearing a leather wrist band—what's this? *This* is supposed to be a bathroom? Three toilets, no seats, two bowls to wash in. Terrible, terrible odor . . . foul-smelling place. Forever stink. Almost want to vomit. Streaked walls, haven't seen paint in how many years? Twenty maybe. Look at those toilets . . . old-fashioned gravity tanks near ceiling, leaking, running down the walls. Those toilets . . . unflushed, stained at the water line. No wonder. Even leaky faucets, dripping, drip, drip; gooseneck pipe leaking, running all over the floor. Floor a mess. Water all over. Where are the towels, no towels.

"Two bowls for a hundred fifty patients?"

"Most of them don't wash, anyway. So it doesn't make any difference."

"Anyone try to introduce the idea?"

"Try it yourself . . . if you want to spend a lifetime around here. It's not easy."

"No, thanks. What else is up here?"

"Nothing. Let's go downstairs."

Same stairs. And me, deathly afraid of fire.

"Only one stair?"

"Yep, just one."

"Ever have a fire drill? Supposing they get trapped up here?"

10

"They can't smoke. How would a fire start?"

"How does any fire start?"

"Look, just between you and me . . . if there was a fire, what would be the loss?"

I can't talk to you, I can see that.

"C'mon this way . . . to the day room."

Another locked door, click, open.

Another attendant, husky masculine female, like she was some guard, which she is, arms folded. Great stone face. Nothing funny in this place, I guess. God, look at this . . . look at it, look at it. See a whole world in a split second. Ugly, unbelievable running sore with four walls. Just like the dorm, dark. Size of a large school room. Big bare square, bare cube. No one would believe this. I could be committed if I tried to explain . . . crowded, jammed with women.

Are these women, are they? How many, how many . . . maybe a hundred. Never saw so many. No one looks at me. Like I was invisible or peeking through a hole in the wall. Step away from the entrance. Do they see me . . . what will they think . . . will my being here start trouble? No, I'm invisible. It's so horrible, I feel like weeping.

Human beings . . . she must be sixty; she, forty-five; that one, twenty maybe; she's fifty . . . cotton dresses, like an acre of drabness. There's a patient's gown, and another, and one on the floor over there, and one there. Yes, and plaid robes, but hanging open. She's naked, and so is she, and so is she . . . she's filthy, been wiping up the floor with herself. Another one naked.

They all look alike. They really look alike, a family from another planet. Impossible, but no . . . a legion of subhumans, with one face . . . anonymous. They look so much alike. Frightful, alien, some other moon. Gaunt, undernourished, starved creatures, stringy unkempt hair, and look at their eyes—now some are looking at me, or through me, at what—sunken eyes, sallow skin, skins, clothes just hang on their bones. Nothing but bones, you be a coat rack, I'll be a coat rack, with eyes . . .

Never saw so many people in one room, not enough chairs, so many on the floor, sitting, lying curled up, apathetically, others standing, looking around vacantly or apprehensively, suspiciously. Look like they're waiting for death . . . with a kind of grotesque patience, for death that never comes. And what are you doing? I am waiting for it to be all over. And you?

Look at them, look. She's jabbering to herself, so is she, at some imaginary enemy, others over there silent, withdrawn, squatting toward the wall . . . staring at the floor, or through it, between their feet, calloused dirty, and bare. That one, emaciated, naked, wrinkled bag of bones . . . they're poking fun at her. What's Nancy doing? Oh, she walks that way, and they skulk away . . . like wolves I saw in a movie.

Idiotic laughing, obscene conversation, current of noise . . . it'd drive *me* crazy in five minutes . . . noise, confusion, laughing. What a hell this is . . . no ventilation, fetid, stinking air . . .

Faded light-tan walls, is that the color? . . . faded tan, streaked with soot and dirt. Lathing all visible everywhere. Walls almost black over the radiator . . . and another in that corner . . .

Dark brown woodwork, never been varnished after put in, I swear . . . plain shades, ugly, that one and that one torn. Pulled halfway down the windows. Screened with heavy wire mesh. No draperies, no curtains, no nothing . . . more bare floors . . .

Furniture here? Only wooden, straight-backed chairs, thirty maybe forty, and . . . and three benches, crude, scarred. Oh, another one against that window . . . not a single thing soft, no texture, no relief. An awful geometry. Stark, starkness. Not even a lamp. Naturally, no flower pots. Always the tip off. No tables, no magazines, no books. Overhead fixtures in ceiling, one globe, one missing . . . just a large, clear bulb . . .

But there's one . . . don't look like you belong here . . . sitting, looking at the floor. Look at her, beautiful, flowing red hair. She's cleaner than the others. Looks at me, sees I'm different from the rest in some way. Looks away again. What are you doing here? Belong here? No. If no, horrible mistake. Doesn't move. Looking down. Neat. Good shape . . . hands, legs, has shoes on. Red hair, dark red, flowing, dropping on shoulders, almost to waist. Holds onto comb. Knuckles white from tight grip. Tight white. What're you doing here? Young. Younger than the rest.

"Nancy, who's that girl? The redhead?"

"Name's Aretta something. Aretta, Aretta Fleming. Why?"

"Looks different from the others."

"Yeah, I know . . . came in two days ago."

Two days ago?

"Two days ago? From where?"

"How should I know?"

That's right, how should you know anything? I'll check her chart later when I have time. Maybe just quiet now . . . never can tell . . .

"Nancy, why is it so many have nicks and scratches on their arms and faces? Even that one. She's got a cut on her nose. And that one, all over her legs."

"Rat bites probably."

"You're kidding."

She shrugs.

"Is that true?"

"I told you."

"The next thing will be bubonic plague."

"What's that?"

What's that.

"Never mind . . ."

Now what? Trouble on top of chaos? What's all that commotion? Everybody crowding to that corner. Nancy rushing over, and another uniformed attendant, I didn't see her. What's she doing? Looks like she's protecting someone. Look at her swing at those patients!

A woman tied to a chair, her head bowed, in a stupor, body tugging at the restraints. Restraints keeping her in a sitting position. Why is she tied that way?

"What is *this?*"

"The others were bothering her, so I told them to shove off."

Athletic-looking female, like the others. If she hits anyone the way she's swinging that arm, she'll knock them through the wall. Ooh, she cracked that one across the face . . . went sprawling, slammed against the radiator. Must lift weights at home. Look at that arm.

"Yes, but why is she tied that way? Nancy, what is she doing in here?"

"No room in the pheno room, I guess. This is the only place they could put her."

"What's the matter with the dorm? . . . or the tub room?"

"Dorm's closed all day, like I told you. No sense using the tubs, she's calmed down now."

"Supposing she's still tied here at night. You don't leave her here, do you?"

"No. Fenwick made a rule that no one's supposed to stay here all night. So we got to carry her up to the dorm

14

and tie her in bed. It's stupid, if you ask me. I don't see why we can't leave her here. What difference does it make?"

What difference does it make.

"Nancy, they all don't sleep all the time, I imagine. Those beds are so close together. What if they get up and walk around? They might walk all over her."

"They probably do."

"Well, anyway, people come in here at night and clean, don't they?"

"No, not too often."

Not too often? No wonder this room stinks so much.

"We put a broom or a mop in their hands to push around during the day."

"In whose hands?"

"One of *these* women. They got nothing else to do."

"I don't understand. How do you pick them out?"

"There's nothing to understand. We just pick anyone."

"How can you get this place clean that way?"

"Well, I'm not going to do it."

"She sure is out cold, Nancy. What did *they* give her?"

"Probably a dose of pareldehyde."

"A 'dose,' eh? How much is a dose?"

"How should I know? Enough."

A dirty vision shocking me awake. All these women, if not in the tub room or phenobarb room, spend their lives here. Diagnoses don't matter. All the killers, the whole group, all here. Hell's team, here.

"Betty, you can see what the deal is. Some of these animals are really dangerous, and they mix with the rest, pester each other, and fight all the time. That's right. So what're we supposed to do? We spend all day breaking up fights."

Oh, you can talk, too. The way you go about it.

"I can see you've had special training for it."

15

"Don't be so goddamn sarcastic, sister. Wait'll something happens to you in here. You won't think it's so funny."

"Who said it was funny? If I want to find the right way to do something, I won't ask you."

Smart aleck tough, how'd you ever get in here?

"First day, and you're already looking for trouble, just like the rest of you students. The boss'll take care of you."

"Phoebe, knock it off. C'mon, Betty, you've got to see the rest."

"Just a minute. Nancy. What does she mean by that crack?" Think I'd better get things straightened out right now.

"She doesn't mean anything . . ."

I'll bet she doesn't.

"Take it easy, Nancy. I want to look around in here for a few minutes."

"Suit yourself."

Notice that they're all looking now. Don't want to attract too much trouble.

That woman smiling at me, smile at her, she's looking away . . . acts like she's afraid of me. Feel sort of self-conscious. What's that one doing over there?

Not more than twenty-five. Suppose she was pretty once. Just stands there with those . . . what? . . . knitting needles? Fingers moving like pistons . . . nothing else moves except those fingers. Sort of a standup version of Madame LaFarge, but wilder. Look around the room, paying no attention to her fingers, watches the action around her, keeps looking around then back to somewhere in front of her. Those fingers. Ask Nancy.

"What is she doing?"

"Who? You don't have to whisper. None of these bitches will know what you're talking about, anyway."

16

Fine way to talk . . . bad as that, that . . . that's her name? Phoebe.

"That one. Is she knitting?"

"Oh, her? No, she's tatting. That's all she does all day long. Just stands there from morning to night. But you don't have to worry about her. She likes the students. Harmless. She'll probably want to decorate one of your handkerchiefs."

"Well, I'll certainly let her." Glad someone is doing something. If she's so harmless, what's she doing here?

"Suit yourself."

"What's a harmless creature like her doing in this place?"

"Look, I only work here. Don't ask me. Why don't you look up her chart? The real answer is there."

I'll bet it is. But not the one you think.

"But where does she get the thread and handkerchiefs?"

"Oh, she has some relatives visit almost every week. They bring her stuff. Give it to us, and we give it to her each day."

Another one sitting on the floor over there. No clothes. Nose running all over the place. Get pneumonia. What's this? Another bathroom . . . same rotten condition as upstairs. One toilet, no seat or cover, one bowl. God, the odor makes me ill. Enough of this. Oh, oh, another walking around naked.

"Don't they have enough clothes to go around? Why are so many naked? I'd think they'd die of pneumonia."

"You're sure new around here. Some of them have. You can't keep clothes on some of those old biddies. I'm telling you, they're not human beings. Just animals."

That makes me boil. Maybe I'm naive or something.

"Is that so? I suppose if you condition a human being to live like an animal, she'll soon become one."

"Oh, yeah? Just wait 'til you're here for a little while, you'll change your tune."

Every time I open my mouth, you get defensive.

"We might as well go."

"You'll be back. Get used to it."

Locked door.

Which key? This one . . . no, this one.

Click open, open, shut click.

Same depressing corridor. There's light at other end, see crack of it along floor. What's with this Fenwick woman? Some instructions she gives. Offhanded way about her. Well, things can't be worse. That's something.

Another door.

Same key? Yes.

Click open, open, shut click.

What's this . . . Oh, I see.

"Well, as you can see, this is the tub room."

Empty now. One student. I don't know her, desk, two, four, eight, eleven, twelve tubs. Look pretty large. A lot of hydrotherapy. Neat in here . . . room to move around.

"Nothing to see here, I guess. Plenty of action sometimes."

Plenty of action. You talk like a strike breaker.

"The scheduling routine is over there on the wall. I suppose Fenwick told you that part of your work is to keep records."

"No, she didn't."

Didn't tell me anything. I see.

"Probably on the sheet she gave you. Let me see your keys. Yes, you have it, the key to the water closet. You'll have to do that, too. Regulate the water, turn it on and off. Let's go downstairs to phenobarb."

No sign on the door. Locked.

Which key? This one.

Click open, open, shut click.

Sedation therapy. Phenobarbital, she said. Three, seven, twelve again. Think they'd have more beds than this. All full . . . patients lying still, most quiet. Except that one. MD making rounds, two students, oh yes, know them both. Seen him before, too.

"Well, it's at least quieter in here."

"It ought to be. They don't have any choice."

"Oh, I see."

Walk to one of the beds. Patients tied down, restraints on both arms and legs. Those two have had restraints removed, look like they're sleeping.

"Well, I got to get back. I guess you know your way around by now."

"Okay. Thanks, Nancy."

Watch her go. Look at that walk again, athletic, masculine. Glad to get rid of her. What kind of training do these kids get, anyway? I'll stick around here until lunch time. What're they doing? Moving from one bed to the next, bathing patients, giving bed pans. Suppose they feed them when trays are wheeled in.

"This can keep you pretty busy, I guess." Frail blonde, blue-eyed girl in her teens, not twenty.

"It's not so bad, and we go off at three. Time flies."

Look at her work. Methodical. No lost motion. Good training.

"That's right, days only. What happens from three to seven A.M. tomorrow?"

Look. She's taking restraints off that one. Elderly.

19

"Who knows? A couple of attendants show up, but they don't do anything."

"How do you know?" Should she be loosening those restraints?

"Don't worry. You know why by the time you arrive again at seven."

"Oh, no."

"But, yes."

"Doesn't the MD say anything?"

"Not to me he doesn't."

"Aren't you afraid to take those off?"

"No, she, like everyone else here, is given four-and-a-half grains of phenobarb, twice daily."

"Really snowed, aren't they? Look, how long are these women kept here?"

"Well, every week twelve are brought in here and tied down for the whole week—"

"A week?" I don't believe it.

"A week, and without ever getting up. I've been here all week, working on the same ones."

"You mean to tell me that they have restraints on all that time?"

"I guess so. Doris and I are the only ones who even loosen them. Supposed to exercise their muscles. Like I say, you get real busy here."

"This is therapy?"

I don't care if he does hear me. Why give me that menacing look, doctor, this isn't my idea.

"Well, what are you going to do? Change the system? We just follow orders."

"I'm not about to change the system. I don't even know what the system is. What time do trays get here? Mind if I stick around and help?"

"They'll be here in a half hour. No, stick around. We can use you."

Nice to be outdoors for a little while before going back. Central dining hall, better call it central soup kitchen, mission branch. Or slop depot. Takes real practice to prepare food that bad. Shouldn't complain, but two-and-a-half months of poorly planned, no, just plain lousy meals gets tiresome.

Being brought up to eat the food put in front of me helps at times like now. Still, remember, yes, remember, the three of us sitting around the table at home, yes, before Jeff died, the three of us sneaking candy bars, then couldn't eat. You ought to be ashamed of yourselves, half the world starving, mother said a hundred times, maybe a thousand, and you sit there picking at perfectly good food. Might as well sit there, because if you sit there all night you're not leaving the table until you eat . . . how many times that happened. And we ate, and no fooling around about it. No finicky eaters in this house . . .

But still, not so bad as . . . what was that garbage we fed them? Still don't know what it was, watered-down slop, even smelled bad. Big metal spoons, hardly get in their mouths, spilling that vile stuff down their chins and all over themselves . . . good thing, spoons, take forever to eat with a fork, wouldn't have the strength to finish.

And what are those huge trays for? Sections for what, more of the same? In this section, dear, we have gruel, and look what we have in this section, gruel . . . and in this section. Yes, and had to feed that poor Negro lady . . . didn't want to touch the stuff. Tears rolling down her cheeks every time I put the spoon even near her mouth. Screws up her face, like in terrible pain. She knew it wasn't right.

Supposed to be helping them . . . great achievement

21

wheeling in huge warming carts. What a picnic. That's a laugh, warm my foot, but no laugh. Expect something warm, at least nourishing, but cold slop, then cold milk in a tin cup. Need a cast-iron stomach to keep it down, cast-iron heart to prepare and dish it out. And those spoons, for a tribe of giants . . . special delivery from a race of madmen . . .

Back to two stories of no principles. Maybe it is a good thing they don't get outside to see where they're living. Look at it. Now I see . . . that's the day room. Funny, you can't see in too well. One look, and you couldn't get them back in, but not really, I suppose. They wouldn't know the difference. Wonder how much difference they do see. That's something no one can tell, no matter how smart . . .

Fine kick in the teeth to the medical profession, all that rotten news in the paper yesterday morning. Tried to find more today, but not a word. Someone has real influence with the dailies . . . they dropped it immediately. Not the first word . . . didn't even say which institution. But I'd bet anything he was on the staff here.

Making book with the patients . . . why, it's absolutely unbelievable. The people have little enough money without his taking it away from them. Any doctor who has so little to do with his time . . . should be reading medical journals, not the racing form, for heaven's sake. I wonder where he was from? Wellingham? No, couldn't be . . . article said something about his placing bets for patients for at least eight months now.

If the truth were known, he probably didn't place a bet. Have to get mixed up with a bookie, or the syndicate. Be a nice racket, just playing the odds and not showing his face to a bookie. Easy way to pick up a lot of loose cash . . . probably some intern, scraping along, trying to support a wife and umpteen kids. Most of these patients probably wouldn't remember what entries they picked from day to day. But which institution?

Back in, no key this time, no click and click.

What a lobby . . . what was that about psychology of color? Lot of good those college courses are when you can't do anything with them and nobody listens, anyway. Later on, I probably won't listen either. Should try, though, to make them believe in several buckets of good psychology and paint it all over the walls. . . . Better check bulletin board for latest word from our leader.

Let's see . . . more new assignments . . . not for me, though. What's this? Wasn't on board yesterday. Must have arrived at dawn to put it up.

FRONTAL LOBOTOMIES DISCONTINUED
UNTIL FURTHER NOTICE

Frontal lobotomies? That's it. He must be the one. Oh, no . . . couldn't be. No, I don't believe it. Yet, why would they put up such a thing? Why, he's the top dog, or one of them, around here. He's no intern, must be well paid. Why would he be so stupid and ruin his whole career? Well, why should I care? Got enough worries of my own . . .

A Day

There's that other door, across the corridor from Fenwick. Should meet her, what's her name? Benson? Agnes Benson, head attendant. If attendant, she's no R.N., but no matter. Smarter than all the rest probably. Door not locked. That's something. There she is, about forty-five, attractive, I guess, more than anyone said . . . walking to desk. Office small, like a cloakroom, no cloaks. Cloaks? So small . . . desk, chair, table strewn with magazines and, yes, pile of work sheets. Book on desk, lying open, upside down, small index card file. Bare walls, one picture, faded something or other, watercolor. One little picture high on the wall.

You certainly moved to your desk in a hurry. What's the matter, unsociable or something, only one chair in the room. What is this? Well, I'll have to stand. Musical chairs for two; you always win.

"Hello. Are you Miss Benson?" Well, say something, you've had your look. Good and long, too.

"Miss Seward, I believe. I expect you will get some valuable experience here . . . It takes a great deal of it to learn how to handle these people."

"Yes, I can see that it does."

You wouldn't kid me, would you?

"How long have you been here?"

"This is my second day."

"I mean at Wellingham."

"Oh, for about two and a half months."

"I see. I've been here for twenty-two years."

Twenty-two years? That's fantastic. How . . . and just this in all that time?

"You look surprised, Miss Seward. Does it surprise you?"

"No . . . no. It isn't that. It's just a long time, to me."

Why don't you look at me when you're talking? Fidgety pencil.

"You mean, I look it?"

Having a hard time being friendly. What are you nervous about?

"No, you *don't* look it. That's just it."

Brown, natural wavy hair, small, thin features, well-formed.

"It's the truth . . . twenty-two years."

Why do you keep fidgeting with that pencil? Every time you see me looking at you, you put your hands in your lap.

"Well, Miss Seward, you're not exactly new to the work."

"No, but this is a little different."

There's that pencil again.

"What do you think of the place?"

Tighten your lips frequently . . . nervous. What difference does it make to you what I think of this place?

"I like the work."

"Nice to see you, Miss Seward."

"I'll be in the tub room today, Miss Benson."

Fingers, fingers.

"Fine. I'm sure we'll get along very well."

How do you know that?

Close door. Seemed friendly enough, if a trifle forced. Just couldn't catch her eye more than a second or two at a time.

Get out the key, which? Yes.

Click open, open, shut click. Well, still quiet. Start here tomorrow. Should get acquainted with that other student. She's still writing. Walk over, see who she is at least.

"Hello."

"Hello . . . I'm Betty Seward. I guess I am to be assigned here for awhile . . ."

What is that noise? That noise? Voices screaming, yelling, like sounds of furniture falling or people bumping walls. Terrible, screaming, violent commotion . . . cursing, bumping, bumping the walls, or floors! Yelling, many voices . . . who is that screaming? At the door, bumping, turning the knob, rattling it. Key in, click open . . . thrown back, crack plaster further . . .

Miss Benson! Same woman? Transformed! Who is she screaming—

"Don't fool with her, goddamn it! Get her down here!"

Who is it? My Lord! Don't move too close . . . just view down the corridor. What are they doing? Doing? Lord, they're dragging that woman along the floor . . . filthy . . . dragging her this way, in here. That's Phoebe, and that other one. Woman jabbering, kicking, screaming. I never heard such screaming. . . .

Oh, she's breaking away, scrambling on hands and knees, back, back, away. Caught her. Why, she kicked her, vicious kick in the back, lumbar. She curses them. Breaks away again . . . no, no. They keep kicking her . . . never heard a human voice that high. High-pitched screaming . . . scratched Phoebe's leg, tearing her uniform. Why do they keep kicking her? Pick her up, heaven's sake, pick her up . . .

"For chrissake, get her in here!"

Now Benson's screaming . . . can't believe it, just talked with her. Same woman?

26

Dragging her all the way! Must be, must be fifty, no, thirty, yards. Get back, Benson . . . no, no . . . they're pulling, dragging her through the door. Benson, don't! She's kicking at the poor creature. Oh, kicked her head against the floor, must have killed her. Look at her, head bounced, bounced off the hard wood, still struggling, screaming, I never heard such screaming. Lord . . . what should I do . . .

Didn't seem to bother her, can't believe it. Get out of the way, must get out of the way . . . against the wall. Don't want to get mixed up in this . . . horrible, horrible. How can they?

Look at her, look at her, look . . . filthy dirty, dragged, beaten, human scrub rag. Look at her, face twisted in terrible anguish, lips, mouth bleeding.

What can I do? What can I? Trying to stand her up. Won't. Keeps pulling, screaming. Benson, Benson . . . animal . . . they're holding her, Benson tearing, tearing her clothes off. Trying to keep them on. Everyone yelling, rushing her to tub, that one. Where's the student going . . . water closet. Water, yes, water, must remember if I have to do it. Look at her, filthy, filthy, cotton shreds of clothes all over the floor, lying in pieces and rags. Still trying to keep them on . . . reaching desperately for a piece, then another. Contest of horror, who can yell the loudest, first prize to everyone, Benson, maybe . . . animal in white and stockings.

Benson picking her up, viciously grabbing her around the waist, skin bag over bones, still fighting madly against, clawing the air, anything. Benson, Benson, what are you doing? Triumph of temper. Throwing her into, not quite, now into tub, over the side . . . ooh, God, scraping her thigh, hip, side against ledge. She's shrieking even louder, impossible, yet louder, piercing, crying they're murdering her. What can I do, what can I do? Nothing, nothing, Lord, nothing. They *are* murdering what's left of her . . .

I am part of this. I am here, on the safe side, here, on the sane side. What is sane? Who is? Either way, like crawling into a bad dream and can't get out again. . . .

Look at Benson, look at her, look, look. Rage is dying, dead, takes deep breath, another, another, calm again, smoothing skirt, looking about calm. Pass the salt and pepper, Miss Benson, in this world of kindness, this gentle world. Walking away, toward the door. Stops, looks at me, why me? . . .

"One of the chronics."

She says calm. Yes, look at me, Miss Benson, and pass the salt and pepper. What else would you like to say? Say something to that pulp of statistic, why don't you? Do what the water can't do, or have you tried? And smooth your dress for the next dance.

But, no, out the door, close click, footsteps away. Sixty, maybe ninety seconds of your precious time and back to your paperback. Yes, maybe ninety seconds like a lifetime of agony and reprisal for being born. Look, look at the statistic . . . she's babbling incoherently, looks at me, then frantically at the ceiling, attendants, me, walls, babbling . . .

Canvas on now, completely covers her, except head. Statistic now a head, scraggly hair and ashen skull. She keeps it up, babbling, on and on . . . hysterical search for peace . . .

What are those attendants . . . that Phoebe again . . . they mock her . . . why, why . . . laughing coarsely, obscenity and obscenity . . . foul mouths, filthy minds. What are they doing? Why, they're provoking her. Phoebe running to bin, what, wet towel, she's throwing it, *throwing* it at her. Hitting her, splash across the face, wrapping around her head. Shriek, shriek. Laugh you maniacs . . . wrong one in the tub. That's the end. Can't stand here like a dummy in this hell any longer. They'd kill her if I walked out. Tub, tub.

"Why don't you leave her alone?" Get the towel off, calm her somehow, miserable wretch. "There, there, . . . no one's going to hurt you. That's all right, there, there . . ." Get rid of this . . . clean towel, where, here. "Here, we'll fix your hair . . . isn't that better?"

Too bad no comb. Use this towel . . . face covered with dirt, blood all over your face, crusted on mouth . . . you two can stand there menacingly all day . . . blood under nose. Nose broken? No. There, that's better. Stand here, maybe stroking her head will help. Christ, what *will* help?

"Smart aleck student . . . buttinski, stickin' her nose in where it don't belong."

"Interfering, you know that, don't you? You'll last about two minutes around here . . ."

More brazen animals than I thought.

"We'll see about that."

Keep stroking her head. Think she's beginning to respond. No. Maybe.

"We're supposed to do a job around here and—"

"Then do it, goddamn it, and stop acting like a couple of gorillas!"

Can't mince words with these two, can see that.

"Benson'll ride your tail right outa here, you'll see."

Wish I was forty pounds heavier, or a man, I'd push her face in.

"If you have any complaints, just make sure it's a threesome when you see your friend."

"Kiss my ass."

That's about your speed, girlie.

"I'll quote you."

Out the door, bang it harder, shut click . . . why doesn't the other leave? Oh, no, she has to stay . . . yes, sit in that chair and sulk. Great for the patients. Symbol of help and authority tearing itself to pieces before their eyes . . . they can understand that, I'll bet. . . .

She's quieting, I think. Get her a glass of water, might help. "There . . . more?" Sure gulps it down . . . what a wreck, and life hangs on in spite of everything, no brain, no will, no reason to go on, and life hangs on . . . she certainly seems grateful. Yes, she's quieter . . . water swirls on, swirls on, on . . .

A Day

These last three days certainly been quiet in here, only two chronics yesterday . . . and Benson, each time, falls apart at the seams . . . ought to have a private tub room just for the staff, with a few clubs and a brickbat or two just to make it feel like home. Could hang a needlepoint picture on the wall like the Steig cartoon or Thurber or whoever it was, "Goddamn our home." Nice personal touch . . .

Now, today just that one chronic, real repeater. Sure she was pretty when she was younger, hardly know it, though . . . couldn't be more than thirty-five. She's a quieter already . . . let me see, two hours in there . . . head not moving around so much. Look at that hair, getting thin, hasn't been washed in a year. How could she, no soap. Wouldn't anyway, I suppose.

Good chance to catch up on all this reading matter . . . shouldn't have stayed up so late last night going over that outline. Wanted to get those behavior studies done.

Now these charts, this is the tenth batch I've brought ten in, I guess, from Fenwick's office . . . still pretty hard to tie names to these histories . . . only know a few so far. Bet I've asked her a million questions . . . some pest she thinks I am. Certainly doesn't have too much to say. I might as well keep my mouth shut.

Strange how they pound us over the head around here . . . learn terminology to understand diagnoses. From the first day, I keep hearing the same thing over and over:

schizophrenic chronic undifferentiated type . . . short for I don't know . . . now, the same thing here. Must have read through seventy-five histories so far . . . everyone has a ream of student observations, like this one . . . who reads these things? Not a mark on them. Sixty-five or seventy of them schizophrenic chronic undifferentiated type . . . even on some of the trusties walking around outside. Pretty common mouthful of uncertainty. This month it's s.c.u.t., next month it's s.c.u.t.

Peculiar, I don't see a mention anywhere—in fact, I haven't heard anyone mention since I arrived at Wellingham—of anyone using Reserpine, or what's that other one, Chlorpromazine. Such a big deal, if you believe the stories, make great strides with these drugs . . . that's what I get for reading magazines. Probably never heard of it in this building . . . but how come not in other departments? And another one, Serpasil . . . not a mention anywhere . . .

Who *does* read these things? Students probably end up reading each other's reports, and that's the end of it. Well, here's one, schizophrenic, catatonic type. That's a switch. Spend a year around this place just out-guessing my classmates . . . no, not a mark on them.

Heaven's sake, here's one of mine . . . just turned it in day before yesterday, no, yesterday morning. Fast work, someone doing the filing. Probably could slip in an old letter or some recipes and no one would notice. Or care. Think I'll do that before I'm through here. End of year, they will put them in alphabetical order, then drop them off the end of a pier . . . listen to that water, we'd be in a spot if we had to manufacture the stuff . . . tranquilize, tranquilize . . . swirl . . .

Who does read these things, anyway? Beginning to bug me . . . there's something screwy about all this . . . behavior studies in a violent ward . . . come on, Seward, straighten out your head: everyone turns in behavior studies . . . we're not doing them for our own benefit, or are we? If someone is reading them over, even just occasionally, do any of these reports have value. Validity, validity? Thy name is validity. Do they make sense to begin with? How could they under these conditions?

Even my own textbook, which I guess I am supposed to throw away as long as I am here, says something about behavior studies being invalid if patients suffer nutritional deficiencies . . .

Remember reading father's notes before he died. Used to think he was too offhand in his criticism of research projects. Remember, remember . . . he used to talk about possible biochemical reason for schizophrenia, the biochemistry of the body, long before others started writing papers about it. Lot of hot air, these research projects, he used to say, and I'd get mad. Then he'd be impatient with me . . . say that conditions would have to be carefully controlled for the results to make any sense. If you want to do research, he'd say, you have to know something about research.

I'm making this too simple maybe . . . somebody'd clobber me if I just opened my mouth about it. They'd be right, I guess, because I don't know anything about it. But something missing . . . missing link, in a house of missing links, which is not kind, I know. Somewhere.

These reports . . . these and these . . . can't be useful because . . . because all the patients are together all the time. Or almost. Lumped, crammed together like fish in a market. Make any difference, I wonder?

If it makes a difference, how can I find out? Take just one mentally disturbed patient. Doesn't know which end is up anyway . . . wouldn't recognize reality if it were printed on her smock. Is she effected by the behavior of another just like her—not just like her, but just as nutty—who is always in her presence? I'll never get the answer from these clock watchers, but every student who has spent time here . . . how many did I ask last night, ten maybe . . . says the same thing: takes very little commotion in the day room to upset the entire bunch. One word, or argument, from one of the chronics and the whole joint is seething with one huge toothache, or headache . . .

Look at this chart, look, been here twenty-five years. Another, here, chronic agitator, criminally insane. How about this one, in here three years . . . first few months not overly disturbed, no trouble; this year, despite therapy—doesn't say what kind—therapy continually, period of extreme agitation has gotten more and more frequent. Periods in between shorter, shorter . . . last month she attacked one of the attendants. Which one? Doesn't say . . . no, doesn't say . . . wonder who it was? Then she attacked another patient, sent her to the hospital.

Well, there's something wrong somewhere, but I'm a nobody. They're supposed to know more than I do, which doesn't seem to be a lot of course. But, still . . . sounds more like policy than sound practice. No, everyone is thrown together, and I mean thrown, and that's supposed to be all right. Yes, policy, I suppose, so, Seward, shut up and keep your eyes open.

Look at this chart—yes, look at this one . . . scheduled three times last month for "repeats" in hydro. And here's another . . . not scheduled by students, I notice . . . hmmm? If a patient is on a "repeat," she could be in the tub when I come on duty and still be in when I go off duty. That's a lot of water . . .

Here's Cookie's writing . . . tub only agitated patient more. Repeat just the same. That's right, Cookie warned me about that . . . wonder who told her? Not a thing, not a damned thing in instructions. Oh, swell. What did she say? Oh, yes, watch temperature of water, face might flush, temperature would go up. Why didn't Fenwick tell me that? Terrible to think that this is a subtle way to knock everyone off. Well, least I can do is watch the water carefully . . . temperature gets too high, temperature of patient goes up, face flush . . . sleep, deep sleep . . . better check it now . . .

A Day

Last night, bigger success than I thought it'd be. Too big, and that's the trouble. Terrific idea of Cookie's—no, whose was it? I've forgotten. Putting on show for patients. Don't know where we got all those chairs—dug out of storage, I guess. A lot terribly dusty. No one bothered to wipe off, so had room filled with walking, sitting, squirming, giggling dust cloths. That gym ideal, but never used for show before . . .

How'd we ever hit on such a nutty idea? . . . Didn't even know whether any of them would get too excited and out of hand. But, no, most. Trusties though. Big impromptu song and dance show. No time for planning, just threw together. Should have had a few canes and coats with the marshmallow buttons. Really went over big . . . they were like kids at Christmas. How many came up to me afterward . . . ones I see on the grounds everyday. Thanked me over and over, and when would the next one be? So grateful, I am ashamed we didn't do better . . .

Now not so sure it was a good idea. Everyone says it was the first time it was ever done. Never any entertainment before . . . trouble is, they've got their hopes for another night soon, and we'll all be gone by that time. They'll wonder where we went. Like starting a tradition and letting it die before a tradition. No, perhaps we didn't do the right thing. Still, who can just vegetate? . . . Leave the world just a little better than you found it. Or some such useless cliché in light of everything else. Seems impossible that no one ever did it before . . . yes, a big chance, but everything's a big chance.

Oops, lost track of the time. Got to go.

Forgot to wind my watch last night. Still running? Yes, wind though just the same . . . almost run down. Guess it's the right time, yes, just seven o'clock. Keys. Nearly forgot them . . . lucky I got no further than outside my room. Returned. Now here. Still on time, though . . .

Door closed and locked as usual.

Click open, open, shut click.

Marjorie here already . . . yes, that's her name. Cookie met her last week. She must have gotten here earlier. Don't think I'm late. No.

Day just beginning, and there's a patient in the tub already. Check log. Log out of desk . . . hmmm, page thirty-four, thirty-five, thirty-six, six . . . this can't be right. Heavens' sake! This is the same woman who was in when I left yesterday afternoon! No. Is she back in again? I was thinking about this very thing when I left. No, she's not logged out. Oh, no! She wasn't logged out from yesterday morning. Same woman in yesterday morning right after I came on! My God, no! Look at her, look at her. Go over.

"Marjorie, Marjorie! My God, this woman has been in here for twenty-four hours."

"No, she can't be!"

Knocks over her chair.

"Look at her. Quick, get Benson and a couple of attendants . . . I'll unstrap her, quick . . . got your key handy?"

"Yes, . . . see if you can get her out. Don't know if Benson is in yet."

Drops keys. Big help.

"Hurry, Marge, hurry!"

Got to get her out of here. Oooh, canvas heavy as lead. God, look at her face . . . there, got it off. Now, oh, there's Benson. She ought to run—

"I think you'd better call a doctor. We've got to get her to the hospital!"

Well, don't just stand there . . . get over here.

"You know, we never call an MD except in an emergency. What's the matter with her?"

"What's the matter with her? Look at her! It's a wonder her skin hasn't peeled off! Looks like a lobster. Look at her! She's in a coma!"

Stupid female, open your eyes.

"Now, don't get so excited, Seward . . ."

Here come those two attendants. Miss Fenwick. Lucky she's here, too.

"Here, you girls, help Miss Seward . . . take her out of there and put her on that stretcher. Get that stretcher. Better take her into the dayroom . . ."

"Dayroom? In this condition . . . Miss Fenwick, look at her."

Kneels over patient. Fenwick, Fenwick . . .

"Let me see."

Taking her pulse. At least enough sense to do that. Wiping her hand over forehead.

"She practically radiating heat. You're right, Seward, she's in a coma. Benson, call Wallace."

Yes, and be quick about it. Better check that log once again. Should be a phone in here, but no . . . it figures. Benson moving like a snail . . . get going, Benson.

"And Benson, . . . come back here when you've called."

Hope Fenwick isn't telling her that for my benefit. Might as well save her breath. Let's see. No, I was right. No other entries . . . twenty-four hours. My God, my God . . .

. . . yes, that's right, Fenwick, about time you came over here.

"Let me see the log, Miss Seward."

Take out of desk drawer . . . there, open to the exact page. It's all yours. Step aside. Picking it up, running finger down page, frowning. You ought to frown. Find it? No? Neither did I. Never checked out. How do you like that? Well, say something . . . is that all you're going to do? Back in the desk drawer? Why, you . . . cover the corpse with a mountain of flowers, and for all the flowers, the corpse is still there.

"Won't the doctor want to see this?"

"If he wants to see it, he'll ask for it."

Don't look at me that way . . . he'll see it. I'll see to that. Pull the drawer half-open.

"You needn't do that, Seward, it belongs in the desk drawer, and that's where it stays."

Is that so? Oh, oh here he comes. Must have been nearby. Haven't seen him before. Glasses, round steel rims, like the front end of binoculars . . . tall head and thick face and hair, that hair, take off the fur hat. Why don't you wear a clean gown? Looking at Fenwick.

"What seems to be the trouble here?"

"Thought you better come over, Bernie . . ."

Oh, it's 'Bernie', is it? Better walk over . . . not going to be left out of this.

"Hmm . . . how long was she in?"

"Can't say for certain."

Oh, yes? I'll answer for her.

"Twenty-four hours, doctor."

"Who are you?"

"Betty Seward, Doctor." Don't try to intimidate me, Fenwick.

"Twenty-four hours? That's impossible. She'd be dead."

It's a miracle she's not. Don't look at me that way, Benson. You either, Fenwick.

"Katherine, is this true? Twenty-four hours?"

"I think there was a mistake in the log . . . she couldn't have been in that long. Miss Seward, don't you think there was a mistake? You're sure you didn't forget to check her out?"

"No, I didn't forget." You won't get out of it that easily. "She was in yesterday morning. Do you want to see the log? It's in my handwriting. I went to lunch, and when I came back, she was still in . . . scheduled for a repeat, I guess—"

"What do you mean, you 'guess'?"

"I mean, Doctor, that I didn't schedule her, so someone else must have—"

"Why must they have?"

"Well, if they didn't, then the attendants forgot to take her out . . ."

Wallace looking around, forced his hand. They love me, I can see that. Big silence.

"So, when I went off at three-thirty, she was still there."

"I see. Katherine, let me see the log. Here, call an ambulance, Benson. Have her taken to the main building, emergency. Tell them I'll be right over."

Fenwick getting the log. Slams drawer shut. Mad as hell at me. Don't care. They know I'm right. Wallace looking at it. Gives back. Leaving.

Keys.

Click open, open, shut click.

Look at Majorie, scared to death . . . well, say something. Better fix canvas. Poor creature. Hope she'll be all right.

"Miss Seward, I want to see you in my office right away."

Going toward the door.

Keys again.

Click open, open, shut click.

Gotten off to a fine start. Not here more than a few days and stirred up half the staff. Why did you do it? You're not a troublemaker . . . I was spoiled at Fulton . . . why did you do it? Fenwick is seething . . . what's this "Bernie" business? Well, I guess they can know each other. I shouldn't care. But he comes on the ward wearing a dirty gown . . . looks like he was changing a tire. And now she's seething mad.

Key here.

Click open, open, shut click.

There they are standing in her doorway. He leaving . . . she going in and closing the door. After she saw me, too. Why don't we have regular MD rounds?

Not locked. Get it over with. Door open . . . looking in the mirror again . . . closed.

"You want to see me, Miss Fenwick?"

"Seward, what do you think you're doing?"

"I don't know what you mean."

Oh, oh, already I can see that was the wrong thing to say.

"You know very well what I mean! Are you trying to prove something? We've had your type before. You come in this place, and the first thing you do is violate the rules."

"I violated a rule?"

"*My* rules. Students are here to learn, not to usurp my jurisdiction . . ."

Because I'm alert, I break your rules.

"You were interfering."

41

Stay out of trouble. She can make things rough. Play dumb.

"I wasn't interfering, Miss Fenwick. The doctor asked me a question, and I answered him."

"Now, you listen to me. Don't be cute with me, young lady. You stuck your nose in where it didn't belong. I say there was a mistake in the log . . . how dare you contradict me?"

"Miss Fenwick, if there was a mistake in the log, it was an omission."

"How can you prove that woman was in the tub for twenty-four hours?"

"Miss Fenwick, it wasn't *my* mistake."

"You're not here to discuss the policies of this institution with me. Hereafter, your contact with the doctors will be made through me. Is that clear?"

"But if you're not here . . ."

"Seward, stop splitting hairs. Emergencies are rare in this building. I ask you, is what I say clear?"

"Yes."

It's not clear at all. It was no mistake that the patient was in a coma.

"That's all. Go back to duty. Lock the door after you."

"Miss Fenwick, I don't have a key to the door."

"I don't *mean* that one. The other one."

A Day

Everytime one of those women wants to talk to me, it's like meeting a friend on the street in the sunshine . . . but not able to talk about the weather. How many times we fall back on weather . . . isn't it a beautiful day. Yes, it is. No rain. Lovely skies. Fresh breeze. Dull but wonderful starter. Brings us together just a little. All born under the same sun. Can't mention it to any of these, though. Or can I? What do say to them? Wonder if any know what day it is? Month? Year? No, of course not. But no difference . . .

Better check dayroom before downstairs to pheno. Entrance lobby. Bulletin board. Yes, pheno again today. Seward, phenobarb Chapman Hart Koch. Koch phenobarb. Work with Cookie again, her last week. Better check dayroom . . . keys, this one.

Click open, open, shut click.

Shades still drawn. There's that smart aleck Phoebe, sitting like a wind-up robot in her chair. No one's wound her up yet, so shades still drawn. Darkness on top of darkness. Same brutal mind. Infinite.

. . . there, this one, now two more. Look at them looking gawking at me, like no one ever pulled shades up. Better to pull their shades down for good if we can't ever pull them up to let in some light.

. . . swallowing my fear, I guess. Different from first day . . . all these mindless souls propped up as if they were fitted to the floor chairs, benches. Come in here, herded in here . . . never have seen that done, come to think of it . . . come down here early. Assume the same places every day then wander about, go back to the same place . . . a quiet limbo. Then sometimes not so quiet. Throw in a few shrieks and yells just to keep the old place normal. Then for a hearty laugh, a mess or two to clean up, and break up fights.

That woman on the floor . . . there . . . the stringiest hair in the world, the working end of a tired mop . . . thin, too. What is she doing? She's . . . she's posing. Gathering her bones together for another world. Looks into space as though a mirror in front of her, on a string. Stylish pose . . . rage the style. She smiles, then turns her head to look at, at her hair. Trying to do something with it . . .

. . . licks her fingers, rubs across forehead, pats a few loose strands. Clean mark on her forehead from rubbing wet fingers across. Only clean, and not so clean, place on her spattered face. What's that she takes from her smock pocket . . . smock pock—looks like, yes, two small sticks. No, two matchsticks. Concentrates on them, like she's arranging . . . arranging to draw straws. Not to, three, thee. Drops one and filthy hand retrieves, has to crawl a little . . .

. . . disturbs that other one, naked in her own urine, who . . . she pushes her back. But falls back herself and . . . and knocks over two others standing there! They fall in a heap, cursing. Probably now a fight. No, milady ignores it all like nothing happened!

. . . there, this shade, just one more . . .

. . . picks up stick, match, poses, starts over. Arrange them, now . . . what is she? She's combing her hair with them. Combing her hair? Yes, she's combing her hair! For God's sake. Pulling them through her strings, her matted strings. One sticks there. Thinks she's lost it. Reaches for it . . . searches. Drops the other two. Reaches all over her

44

head, like searching around the room, or around the world. Looks about wildly, afraid that it's gone. There's going to be trouble . . . should help her, but no . . .

Now she finds it. And not a second too soon. Begins again. Arranges matches in fingers like a poker hand, one by one, combs again. Sticks through strings . . . and strings stay strings forever. Until they fall out.

Starting to pose all over again, never tires, and gathering sticks and self together for same world's away audience. As if no walls at all . . . and preparing to endure, endure her isolation over again . . . really the same here as in any world she chooses . . .

In all her bathless, smelly, obscene self, she is true. I resist, she bends, has bent . . . the same fate.

Yes, runny-nosed, dirty old lady, we both, we all, are alone. The same, the very same aloneness. In the beginning, the end, throughout our living. I spend my life reinforcing the illusion that I am not, but I go on because I am curious about the illusion. Who, what, will help me fill it out tomorrow?

Better to bend and no longer know it? Do I admit it now? Do I lead myself to the fact early? Or do I wake up terror-stricken one morning when I'm fifty, find the idea descended upon me, banging me between the eyes?

. . . last shade. Least, a little better, some sunlight. Sunlight doesn't get rid of that smell, though. There's that redhead again, certainly different from the rest. Belongs here? Must check. Sitting there, tears rolling down her face. And the old girl next to her . . . probably not old at all if truth were known . . . probably . . . heavens, what's the matter with her face?

Go over.

Standing in front of her. Redhead moves away.

Looks at me, away, then at me, then away. Hand on shoulder. Oh, startled, jumps back from me.

"Now, now . . . I won't hurt you."

You've been hurt all right, by someone else. You poor thing, bruises all over your face, blackened eye . . . your jaw, swollen, red.

"What happened to you?"

"What . . . what happened to you?"

"No, not to me . . . what happened . . . can you tell me?"

"What happened?"

"How did your face get like that? It hurts, doesn't it?"

"Hurts . . . yes, my face."

Puts hand to face, neck, rubs jaw.

"What happened to you?"

"I . . . I don't know . . . what happened to me?"

Get nowhere this way. Look around. All looking at me. Cross room, to Phoebe, arms still folded. Needs winding.

"Phoebe, what happened to that woman?"

"Which woman?"

"*That* one . . ."

You know which one, you insolent beast.

"How should I know? I just came on duty."

"Wasn't she in restraints . . . yes, I saw her in the phenobarb room yesterday. Wasn't she in restraints."

"Look on her chart. How should I know?"

"Well, dammit, I'm positive that she was. She didn't do that to herself. She couldn't have. Who was on duty?"

"Why don't you look on the duty roster?"

Like a bunch of thieves . . .

"Phoebe, that woman needs some medical attention."

"Better see Benson."

"Where is she?"

"Day off today."

"In the meantime, she sits there, maybe with a fractured jaw."

"What can I do about it?"

Nothing. What else do you do? Better keep my voice down. No sense in starting anything. She'll just have to rot there. Downstairs, Cookie will be waiting. To door.

Key, this one.

Click open, open, shut click.

There's Fenwick.

"Miss Fenwick . . ."

She's ducking into her office.

"Not now, Seward, have an appointment."

Yes, I'm sure you have. Well, I'll just follow you.

"Miss Fenwick, may I review one of the charts?"

"That's what they're there for, Miss Seward. Help yourself. I'll be back later."

Can't get away from me fast enough, can you?

"Where is the duty roster?"

"On the board where it always is."

"No, I mean the attendants'."

I thought that would stop you.

"Seward, why do you want that?"

"I just want to see who was on duty last night."

"It's in Benson office. She keeps it locked. I'll get it when I come back."

And out you go. Well, I'll see if my memory is right. Let's see, Swanson, Stinson, Turner. Yes, Turner. Tenth, eleventh, twelfth. Yesterday was the twelfth . . . phenobarbital therapy. I thought so, restrained all day yesterday. She couldn't have inflicted those injuries on herself. Doesn't know what happened, poor soul . . . place like a modern inquisition, and not so modern.

While I think of it, where's that chart for the redhead? Meant to look up before. Fleming, Fleming. Here. Aretta

Fleming. Schizophrenic, chronic, undifferentiated type . . . here we go again. From County General, Psychopathic Section. Wallace's case. Diagnostic ward, transferred to hydrotherapy. Now here. Why? No mention why. Oh, here it is: attempted suicide. Suicide? Now here?

Better get downstairs. With a few sound effects, they can make this a real horror chamber . . .

Phenobarb room door.

Key out.

Click, open, open, shut click.

"Hello, Cookie."

"Hi, Betty, come here. I want to show you something."

Past several beds. To that Negro lady. Must be over sixty. Could be seventy. What's the matter with her?

"Look at her . . . I checked. Been tied down there over twelve hours . . ."

"God, Cookie, look at her hands."

"Yes, that's what I mean."

Restraints so tight, she's got large blisters, look just like rope blisters, huge blisters on her wrists. Her hands, hands so swollen, it'll take a couple of days to get them down to normal size.

"Cookie, it'll take a day or two to get her hands down to normal. What happened around here last night? You know there's a gal upstairs, Turner, who looks like she has a broken jaw?"

"This isn't the first time. When I came on this morning, the attendant going off . . . I think her name is Gruber, Shirley Gruber—"

"Yes, I know her. She was on days last week—"

"That's her. She was in a terrific temper when I came on. Said about ten of the patients were agitated, and she couldn't quiet them down. So—"

"Oh, Cookie, don't tell me."

48

"In a fit of anger, she must have tied them all down whether they required it or not. Everyone was too tight when I checked just now. Better help me."

"This is a crime, Cookie, what can we do about it?"

"Nothing, I guess."

"You loosen that one, I'll get this one. Who was here with her?"

"I don't know. Shirley was by herself when I came in."

"This is sickening. I certainly didn't bargain for this."

"Who did? Here, better sponge her. I'll get some water."

"Oh, it's you, Seward . . . you wanted to see the attendant duty roster this morning, didn't you? Why did you want to see it?"

"I don't have to now, Miss Fenwick. I found out . . . Shirley Gruber."

"Oh, yes? What about her?"

Stop thumbing through papers and look at me.

"Miss Fenwick, I've just spent a miserable eight hours downstairs—"

"I've been here seven years, Seward, and I can't remember a single day that was too pleasant."

I'm not interested in hearing your story. You've probably made it that way.

"I've spent a miserable eight hours today undoing all the damage that Gruber girl did last night in phenobarb."

"What do you mean?"

You've decided to look up, have you?

"Just that, Miss Fenwick. You should see the condition of some of those patients down there. Every one of them was tied down so they couldn't move a muscle all night. Now they've been frantic all day. We've had to schedule every one for a repeat . . . and more are due but we have no room."

49

"If that were true, Seward, the other girl would have reported to me this morning."

"I'm just explaining to you what we found this morning. Not only that, but that patient, Turner, has been in the dayroom all day without medical attention, and I'm sure she has a fractured jaw!"

"Why didn't you call the doctor?"

"You told me not to unless you knew about it."

"Now, look here, Seward—"

"Miss Fenwick, will you come downstairs with me?"

"I will not! What do you think this is? I'm tired of your interference—"

"Interference?"

"You heard me. If anything was critically wrong downstairs I would have heard about it from the other attendant! I'm going to tell you for the last time, stop interfering with the way I run this ward. I've been watching you. Don't you think I know what's going on?"

Yes, what *is* going on? I can't argue about that.

"Look, Miss Fenwick, won't you come downstairs with me?"

"No! And that's final!"

"Where am I going to put the new group coming into phenobarb?"

"Don't administer repeats."

"But they're already *on* repeats."

"You've been instructed what to do—tie them to chairs in the day room. No, Seward, you had better put them in the dorm. Use restraints. Get a couple of attendants, one from the tub room and one from the dayroom."

"But I'm going off duty now."

"Then what are you worrying about?"

"Will you look at Turner in the dayroom?"

"All right, all right. Just stop being so impudent and leave my office."

I'll leave. Don't worry. I can't stand it for another minute. This is ridiculous. Impudent, am I? And I'm only trying to do a good job.

Key.

Click open, open, shut click.

What is wrong with her? It's not fair . . . why does she have it in for me? Hallway, deserted as usual, private hell with locked doors. Except this one. What difference here? Fresh air, fresh air and sun welcome relief, but for me only. Here comes Janet, working days at the hospital, I think.

"Hello, Janet, off duty?"

"Hi, Betty. Yes. Going back to the dorm. Going my way? Got a date for supper. What are you looking so blue about?"

"Oh, I'm so furious, I could explode . . . trying to do a job . . . more attendant brutality. I report her, and Fenwick treats me like some filthy informer. Oh, well, you know, why go into it."

"Yes, I know, she's the same with everyone."

"But why?"

"How should I know? She just is."

"Wish I could console myself with that."

"Betty, remember what you told me about your trouble in the tub room the other day?"

"Yes? The old gal in a coma?"

"She died this morning."

"No! What reason?"

"Who knows? Hypostatic pneumonia on the chart. Heart failure, too."

"That's like someone strangling me, then reporting that my death was caused by asphyxiation. That's all they put down, eh?"

"She never regained consciousness. They can always think up the right words, can't they?"

"Always very official sounding."

"It's a rotten shame. I got in hot water over that, you know."

"Well, she's free, you might say."

"Yes, I guess so. See you later, Janet."

Slammed the lid closed on her life, now nothing but a statistic. Free. Free statistic. Free from beatings, free from towels in the face. Free from this unspeakable indifference, no more rotten luck not having some desperate recourse to protection. No one to turn to even at the last. Just sent on her way with a last beating. Now her family will come and thank everyone for taking care of her. There will be amenities all around, a few lies, a few sighs of relief. A free, free statistic.

A Day

Here comes one of the attendants . . . didn't hear her leave behind me. No click, open. Takes the crosswalk . . . sees me . . . comes back . . . comes back. Heading this way. Now what?

"You're the new student I've been hearing about."

Smiles at least. Guess she's not going to hit me.

"I suppose so."

"I was walking over to the coffee shop in the main building. Wondering if you'd like to join me?"

"Yes, yes, I will. I have a little time."

"You're Betty Seward, aren't you? I'm Gloria Hansen. I've seen you coming on duty, but I guess we haven't worked together."

Working together: that's one way of putting it. Big blonde. Tall as I am, but bigger. Steps right along. Along.

"No, we haven't. Saw you a couple of times in the pheno room when I went downstairs to see a friend of mine."

"Oh, that's right. Cookie. I'm there most of the time, occasionally in the dayroom."

"On days?"

"Yes, mostly. My husband is a G.I. over in Germany, so since I'm alone, I like to get home when it's still light."

"Don't blame you. Of course, I'm living here until my affiliation is up. Might as well, too far to get home every day. What've you been hearing about me?"

"Oh, a lot of rough talk, naturally, but I gather most of it is because you make the mistake of trying to do a good job."

"That's a mistake?"

"Here, it is. Don't get me wrong. You're not the first one. Everyone tried to do a job at first, until they get the idea beaten out of them—"

"Beaten out is the right word."

"Psychologically, I mean, which is better than physically. I've got scars to prove it."

"I don't even get a decent 'hello' out of anyone there, and you're the first who's talked to me. How long you been here?"

What does she mean, scars to prove it?

"Oh, about eight months. Here, let's go in here."

"All right. We can sit here. What would you like?"

"No, Betty, I'll get it. It was my idea. Coffee? Cream? Sit tight. I'll pick it up."

This'd be a great place to try out some of that WVW food. They could give it away, and we'd still get some action. She said she's in the pheno room most of the time. That's where Cookie is having so much trouble. Was she the one? No, it was that idiot, Shirley Gruber, I think. But where was she all the time? Well, I won't start an argument with her, not today at least . . . I'm tired . . .

Oh, oh, here comes Fenwick and, and that doctor friend of hers, wearing his garage mechanic gown. Why does he keep wearing that rag? . . . aren't there any coats in medical stores? It's like so many other things around here I don't understand . . . I do, and I don't . . . like scrubbing for surgery, then going out in the street to play a little stick ball. Not very much, just a little stick ball.

Did she see me? . . . probably did, but avoiding me . . . watches him eat as if something to see. It *is* something to see . . . eats sandwich and whole face fluid flesh. Heavy, loose, leathery cheeks move, lips, forehead, ears move, chin . . . that's right, chew with your ears.

Coffee.

"Thanks, Gloria. No, black is all right."

"Just saw Fenwick."

"Yes, I saw her. Don't look now, but she's doing a double take. Aren't you afraid of your job, sitting with me?"

"Hmmph. No, they need us peons too badly. Otherwise, they'd have to go back to work."

Now she's really looking this way . . . probably thinks I'm poisoning her employees.

"Gloria, what were you saying about scars? Were you just kidding?"

"No."

Drinks.

"No. I wasn't just kidding."

Drinks some more. Sorry I asked.

"Betty, I am just as sick as you are of the treatment handed to these patients. But I have to admit, it's a terrible confession—I am probably as responsible as anyone. When I first came here, well, I used to be the way you are, having a feeling of sympathy of these godforsaken women—"

"Why did you come here to start with?"

"Oh, like so many, full of clean ideas, naive hope. Putting in my time behind a steno pad while my husband's away just didn't make any sense. Didn't know what I was getting into, but I'm going to stick it out—"

"Excuse me for interrupting."

"That's all right. What I want to say is that soon after I got here, my guard was down one day, and one of the chronics attacked me. I didn't see her soon enough. She hit me in the neck, and I ended up in the hospital for a week. I was furious, of course, and when I got out, I was filled with stupid revenge.

"But I've cooled off. The point is, and there's no sense in your learning it the hard way, while you're here, it's either your neck or theirs, and it's not going to be mine anymore. Pretty soon you get to spot the real troublemakers, and you stay away from them."

"I know that. But that's not my complaint."

"I know what your complaint is. It's the same as mine. But we could sit here all day and speculate about it, couldn't we? What good would it do?"

One more voice resigned to silence. If we could add them all together, they'd make quite a racket. Well, maybe not.

"I'll tell you something, though. Naturally, nobody's going to listen to me, just an attendant, and I don't know much. But one thing I've really learned in that ward, and it's been a terrific lesson. And that is, except for the women who are almost always violent, if you walk away from a patient who is temporarily violent, she'll quiet down. Sometimes you think you can't afford to walk away, that they'll stir up everybody, but it works.

"Some of the high-priced talent around here will say I'm nuts, but they haven't been on the ward day-in and day-out like I have. For some reason, anyone's amateur psychology is scorned around here, but it's better than breaking an arm or crushing someone's skull. In fact, there'd be less broken bones if some of those kids would walk away.

"And it isn't that any little thing is going to do a world of good or *any* good. No, that's not it at all. But we're there to try to keep peace, and that's one way of doing it. And I've got eight month's time, a helluva lot of hours to prove it. But I can't even get any of these numbskulls to buy my idea—"

"Numbskulls? Who do you mean?"

"Oh, the attendants, of course. They're the only ones who count in there, anyway. What good would it do to tell an MD or Fenwick or anybody who comes and goes?"

Drinks some more.

"Have you been noticing that redhead in the day room? You know, the good-looking one, Aretta Fleming?"

"Yes, I know, Betty. I knew her before she came here."

"You know her?"

"Well, not exactly. I talked to her father when she was committed. Happened to be at court when he appeared, had coffee with him, in fact."

"But I thought—"

"Yes, you thought that only student nurses were allowed to attend?"

"Well, yes."

"I had always wanted to go, so I got permission from the main office."

"Oh, I see. I didn't mean that the way it sounded."

"I know, I know. Well, I was there. You ought to go. Real education."

"What happened to her?"

"Well, it's pretty typical. Her father told me what he knew, which wasn't much. She's only nineteen, comes from Nebraska. Only child. Pampered by her mother. The usual clichés. Told her that she was beautiful, ought to leave their little burg, Kearney or somewhere. Mother died when she was seventeen, and after that, she began to pester her father about going to the big town.

"He said she was obsessed with the idea. And he kept saying, no, so she ran away. Came straight here. Looked around for a job for weeks. Couldn't do much. Of course, he didn't know what she could've been living on. Didn't find anything, and soon she ran out of money. So she goes and

57

gets a job at the Bijou Grand . . . Bijou Grand . . . why is there a Bijou something or other in every town?"

"The Bijou Grand? A burlesque house?"

"Oh, yes. Her father said she told him she didn't mind being a stripper so long as she made some good money and didn't have to trot through the manager's back office or bedroom or whatever. Of course, he didn't put it that way."

"I imagine he didn't. Well, sounds very simple."

"Very. So when her father found out about it—she had to tell him sometime—he blew a gasket and came here to take her home, I guess. He told me she had changed quite a bit, began arguing with him the minute she saw him. Was really difficult to handle. Couldn't do a thing with her."

"How long since she had left home?"

"I don't know. Weeks maybe. Maybe two or three months. Anyway, he found her so resistive and increasingly difficult that he had to call the police. One night she—"

"What do you mean, he had to?"

"I don't know if he had to, but he did, anyway, and they took her over to County General."

"Yes, I've been over there."

"Then you now what happens. They observed her for a few days. I suppose, and made temporary diagnosis. Obviously, they thought she should be committed."

"Obviously?"

"Well, she's here, isn't she?"

"Yes, yes, I see. Of course."

"I saw her in court that day and met her father. Poor Mr. Fleming went to pieces."

"What is it like, the court I mean. I don't even know what it's called."

"I think it's called—I don't, either—court of inquiry or something. But I don't think it matters."

"No, it doesn't. It exists. I was just curious."

"Betty, you really shouldn't miss it. The sessions are held four times a week, and they call in the family and relatives. The patient isn't brought in at the same time, never sees the person who commits her. And the judge tells the relatives the decision of the doctors. Even asks them if they think it will be all right.

"Well, you can imagine what happens. The family is so befuddled, don't know if they're on foot or horseback. Aretta's father fumbled around: 'If you think that's what we should do, we'd better do it.' Tears running down his face. So he signed a bunch of papers, and they sent her here. Call it a judicial commitment."

"How come here?"

"Mr. Fleming moved here recently. He's a retired farmer."

"Gloria, I know it sounds pretty rough, but what else can they do?"

"Don't ask me. Oh, of course, they are sincere, but the way those guys grind out the cases—a real railroading job. The trouble is, if you don't have a pot full of money to take care of someone in your family who is mentally ill, you're a peasant. You're at their mercy, and you know what it's like here."

"Yes, but what is she doing in WVW?"

"She was put in a diagnostic ward over in the women's building, and your friend, Dr. 'Bernie', who is on the diagnostic board, took over her case."

"Yes, my friend, the one who wears the filthy gowns."

"The same. Anyway, the way I get the story, she made friends with a Negro girl about her age, who was also committed recently. One night the Negro girl had some trouble with one of the attendants, and she was put in restraints. Aretta took her part, and there was a big fight, and she also

59

ended up in restraints. I don't know how it all started, but the next day, they switched Aretta to hydrotherapy ward. She became more depressed and tried to commit suicide. So they put her in WVW."

"Because she was suicidal?"

"Policy, I guess."

"That is really stupid. She doesn't belong here. Any fool can see that. Jammed in with a pack of treacherous females."

"What can you do?"

Now it all ties in. The chart. No mention of the incident. Policy is going to kill her. Kill her. I'm as sure of it as anything I can be. The right hand doesn't know what the left hand is doing.

A Day

There's that Nancy Barnes . . . smart-aleck to infinity . . . haven't seen her since the first day. She's scheduled for the dayroom but here she is, standing in the hall reading a magazine. Might as well go in . . . can do some behavior studies, catch up while I'm standing around, anyway.

"Nancy, are you going in?"

"What for? They don't need me in there."

You don't know how right you are.

"You can suit yourself."

Maybe if you sewed a pocket in your uniform, you could bring the magazine with you.

Keys. Here.

Click open, open . . . she's coming in, I see . . . shut click. Where is the? There she is, the redhead. Face is dirty and hands, too. First time I've noticed. Looks right past me. I'm like all the rest to her already. Hate this filthy pigsty. Like walking into the nightmares of a hundred and fifty separate worlds at the same time. The smell almost makes me vomit. I hear water running in the bathroom. What's going on there? Oh, my God, what's she doing?

"Nancy, will you come here, please?"

"What now?"

Old scraggly woman sitting on toilet bowl, no, in it, leaning into sink . . . she's dripping wet. What's she doing . . . got her arm under water soaking, soaking plaster cast off. Soaking cast off?

"Oh, not again? Goddamn it, that's the third time she's done this."

Yanks her away from sink, she falls onto floor, right into puddle . . .

"Watch what you're doing, Nancy. Help her up. Her, that's it."

Winces, but doesn't cry out. Stand her up, collapses again . . . gooey plaster stopping up drain. It's all over the place, what a mess . . .

"Oh, all right. We ought to leave the cast off for awhile, just to teach her how to live."

"Don't be ridiculous. How did she break her arm in the first place?"

"Don't ask such a stupid question, Seward."

"Better get an ambulance. Call the hospital."

"Aw, shit, let her stew for awhile. See how she likes it."

"Are you going to call, or do I have to do it?"

"I'm going."

"I'll wait here for you."

Third time she's done it, eh? It'll take fifteen minutes now to get the ambulance here, to take her once more to the infirmary . . . like some gigantic treadmill. If they'd watch her, she wouldn't get a chance to do it. Wonder who's got the plaster contract for this place, need a lot of it . . . compounded by an attendant breaking her arm pushing her into hydrotherapy . . . that's what Cookie was talking about at dinner . . .

. . . couple more in here, at least. Let's see, that one with her left foot wrapped like a balloon, and that one, left foot, too, plastered all the way to her knee. Plaster cast and no clothes. If they broke enough of her bones, she wouldn't need clothes—be covered with plaster. Open season on left feet in here. Attendants cut in on the plaster consumption. With a little practice, we can get them all in that so-called bathroom, have a party, by the numbers, soak off. One, soak, soak, two.

Here comes Nancy again. Oh, oh, didn't lock the door. That's why several walked over there . . . out the window, there's Wallace coming up the walk. Want to see him.

"Nancy, watch her for a minute, will you? I see Wallace coming in. I want to see him."

"What about? He knows all about this."

"No, never mind about this. No doubt he does know. I'll be back in a minute."

Keys. Here.

Click, open, open, shut click.

Here he comes.

Don't care if they throw me out of here, I'm going to corner you about the Fleming girl. A whole week's gone by, and you've left her in that hell hole. Never saw a human being go downhill so fast. Everyone can say what they want about these people not being in touch with reality . . . the reality of this place is having a terrifically bad effect on her. She shouldn't be in there. She shouldn't. Shouldn't—

"Dr. Wallace . . . Dr. Wallace."

Gives me that pleasant patronizing grin of his as if I wanted to pass the time of day. You know what I want . . .

"Doctor, has anyone spoken to you about the Fleming girl? Don't you think—"

"Why, yes, Miss Seward. Two or three of the girls have already mentioned her. What's the trouble now?"

"Well, there's no trouble. It isn't that."

"What is it, then?"

Don't interrupt me like that, you fool. Let me finish. Take that smile off your face.

"I was just wondering if she shouldn't be transferred out of this ward. She's changed for the worse this last week.

Already she's shown signs of personal neglect. She was so neat when she came here—"

"Now, don't you concern yourself with her . . ."

If I don't, who will?

". . . I've been observing her. I'll arrange a transfer for her if she seems to get worse. She needs very close supervision."

"Well, all right, if you say so."

That's right, turn and walk away quickly. Fur hat for hair slapping up and down on your head. If she seems to get worse. What are you talking about? You're not blind . . . if you know she needs close supervision, you're just burying her here. You don't care. Crowded in thee, in all that filth, noise, cackling, shrieking, screaming, yelling, filth. She gets worse by the minute . . . and every minute's an hour here. Can't do anything else, I guess, except put it on her chart. Must make note that I called his attention to her over and over again. Even if the food were better, that would help. Wish I could really do something . . . wished it a thousand times. Will get that chart right now.

Fenwick's office.

Key. Here.

Click, open, open, shut click.

They'll need another clipboard for Fleming's charts by the time I'm through. It's worth it . . . she seems the only one worth saving at this point. But better get back to the day room where I'm supposed to be . . . that's the next thing Fenwick'll hit me with, being away from duty . . . before Nancy starts complaining.

Keys here.

Click, open, open, shut click.

One, two, three . . . six, seven, steps to hell again . . .
. . . key.

Click open, open, shut click.

As long as I was in hydro or in pheno, I could keep the nightmares in order. One or two at a time. But so overwhelming here, will never clean my mind out. I see ambulance got here. Well, they'll set her arm one more time.

"The old lady's gone, I see."

"No such luck. They just took her to the hospital to fix her cast."

"No, I mean they came and got her."

"Yeah. That old bitch is really bugging me. The next time it ought to be cement . . . then drop her in a sewer."

"You'd do that, wouldn't you?"

"You're goddamn right I would. I don't know why they keep any of these hags around here."

That's right, make up your own rules. Everyone wants to do that, anyway, and not just here. Ignore her. What can I do while I'm here? Look around. Oh, yes . . . now, I've wondered about that one by the window.

"Nancy, what about that little old lady by the window? I've *never* seen her with any clothes on."

"If you want me to stand over her with a club, I'll keep them on her."

"Your usual miserable attitude."

"Well, she just won't keep them on, that's all."

Maybe she won't . . . well, have nothing else to do, I might as well try. Get a clean smock out of stores.

"Be back in a minute."

Key.

Click open, open, shut click.

Linen stores over here. Key. This one. Click open, open. Smallest uniform I can find. This one . . . all right. At least, she's keeping her shoes on. Shut click.

Back to dayroom . . . like heartbreaking zoo to unlock

and lock . . . except other animals have breathing room and are kept safe and healthy by well-paid keepers.

Key.

Click, open, open, shut click.

There she is standing like soft stone except once with dreams, plans, love, vanity . . . she sees me and turns her back.

"Here . . . I have something for you . . . a very nice dress."

Throws both arms up as if I am going to hit her . . . won't let me come near her.

"Here . . . here, I have something for you, something nice, this beautiful dress."

Falling on her knees . . . this naked wreck, wrinkled carcass, holding her hands and arms over her head to protect herself . . .

"I'm not going to hit you. Look at what I have for you."

She peeks from her cave. Not the first to fall, collapse, not the last. She kneeling here, the rest at any time now. I could kill her, kill them all, and they would be free . . . free from this, yes, and I am ashamed even to think it, free from our grand protection.

"Here, I have something very nice for you."

Gets off her knees, suspiciously, terror all over her face.

"Take care of, take care of the Arnolds."

"Let me help you." Doesn't seem to object now. Wish it were quieter in here . . . babbling would drive anyone nuts. That's right, beautiful and clean. There, one more button. "Now, doesn't that look nice? How nice you look."

Will wait now to see what happens.

Fifteen minutes, and she still stands there, looking down at herself. Oh, I was afraid of that . . . starts to unbutton.

Now it's off again, and we're back to the beginning. I won't push it. Let's see what happens tomorrow. Nancy, smirking . . . jerk smirk. The hell with her. I've got a theory about this, so we'll see.

A Day

What's this note from Cookie? Superintendent of nurses?

"Fairchild wants to see you right after you get off duty. She seemed mad about something. I thought she was going to hit me, she was so mad. Said to make sure that you came to her office today, not tomorrow. Give me all the gory details at supper."

Now what did I do? From the sound of this note, I won't be around for supper. I thought things were pretty peaceful in WVW. Haven't seen Fenwick in a couple of days . . . don't even go in her office to read charts anymore, since doesn't do me or anyone else any good, anyway. Superintendent? I hardly know her . . . haven't said hello to her more than three or four times since here, eight, nine and half weeks . . .

. . . her office, over by the fence . . . there's Mr. Monroe still cutting bushes with invisible clippers, will avoid him this afternoon. That lopsided world you're looking at, Mr. Monroe, is not your world, it's mine.

What could she be so made about? No keys here, anyway. No click open. Second, third, fourth office, name on door, Miss Ethel Fairchild, ee, eff.

"Did you want to see me, Miss Fairchild?"

"Yes, I certainly did, Miss Seward. Come in and close the door."

Will stand up.

Seems calm. Quiet before the tornado. Heavy woman,

waist pushes against her belt, round head and flat face except that . . . that meaty nose, pinched at the bridge by years of pince nez glasses . . . pinched by pince. She walks to filing cabinet, puts away folder, looks out window, walks her heavy step to desk, meaty nose jiggles with vibration. Now looks at me and wipes hand across face like a man and jiggles that nose some more.

Points to chair.

"Sit down, please."

"Yes, ma'am."

"What newspaper does your brother work for?"

"What newspaper?"

"Yes, that's what I asked you. You do have a brother, don't you?"

"Yes, but he doesn't work for a newspaper."

"Oh, come now. Let's not start playing these games. What newspaper?"

"Miss Fairchild, I don't know what you're talking about."

"I've gotten quite an earful about how he's going to straighten things out . . . expose us."

"Are you sure you are talking to the right person, Miss Fairchild?"

Temperature's rising. Red in the face. That meaty nose jiggling again. What is she talking about?

"That's not the only thing. I'd like to know if your mother has emotional difficulties?"

"Miss Fairchild, will you *please* tell me what this is all about. If my brother did work for a newspaper, what bearing would that have on me?"

"You have a unique way of being evasive, Miss Seward—"

"I'm not being evasive. I simply don't know what you're talking about."

69

"Your mother has been calling you several times each day for the last two days—"

"Mother knows my schedule. When I get off duty, I call her."

"Oh, she knows your schedule, does she? You talk about your duty here at home?"

"Of course. She's as interested in my work and welfare as I am. We talk over the phone almost every day, so she knows when I am off."

"We'll discuss that further in a minute. Since you don't seem to know what I am referring to, I will tell you—"

"Yes, please do."

Oops, said the wrong thing . . . she's glaring.

"Your mother called so often yesterday and today, raising so much of a fuss that the operator referred her to me. Then she proceeded to give me an earful. I seems that you discuss your duty here rather extensively. You find the situation here so impossible—"

"That is not so. I never said that. I was only talking about WVW—"

"Don't interrupt me. It is so impossible here that you've filled her head with a lot of exaggeration—"

"I never exaggerate."

"Miss Seward! Do *not* interrupt me. Your mother blames me and tells me that your brother is going to take these stories to the newspapers—"

"Taking stories to the newspaper and working for one are two different things."

She stops altogether. I think she's going to explode, then I'll have to clean up the mess. I'd better shut up.

Still silent.

"Now, what I want to know is, what newspaper does he work for? And what do you mean by discussing confidential matters outside these grounds?"

I am not going to say another word until you shut up for a minute.

"Are you going to answer me?"

"My brother does not work for a newspaper."

"What does he do?"

"He works for a manufacturer."

"What does he do for them?"

"He's in the purchasing department."

"Then what is your mother talking about?"

"I don't know what she was referring to. The last couple of weekends, I've gone home very discouraged and tired, and when mother asked me what was wrong, I told her—"

"Told her what?"

"I told her what a difficult time I've had trying to do a good job in WVW. I guess she's taken it too much to heart. If I had any idea she was so upset—there's no sense in both of us being upset—I would have tried to calm her down."

"Miss Seward . . . I've been checking your record, and—"

"Is there something wrong with it?"

"No, . . . that's besides the point. You are nearly through your training, and in all that time, haven't you learned anything about the ethics of your profession?"

Don't lose your temper, Seward. Keep calm, don't get thrown out.

"I have learned a great deal about medical ethics."

"Then why do you discuss your practice outside of this institution?"

"Miss Fairchild, I don't discuss my practice outside this institution. If I have discussed anything, it has been the resistance I've met trying to practice decently. I was told to do certain things in that ward, and I did them. I thought that they were to serve some constructive purpose until, until I found out everyone was ignoring me and I was just going through the motions. When I asked if an MD made regular rounds, I was told that it was not necessary except in emergencies. And I have reported emergencies every day, only to be told that I was not to be the judge of what was an emergency—"

"How dare you, young lady. Not even out of training, to set yourself up as a judge of our medical standards?"

"I'm not talking about medical standards. Medical standards? I don't need an hour of training to recognize brutality and criminal neglect when I see it. In fact, Miss Fairchild, I don't need any training at all to tell that those patients are frightened of their very lives. You know as well as I do, some of the chronics have been there for fifteen or twenty years, and now there are just too many mildly agitated patients thrown in with them. They're all in a constant state of nervous tension."

I think she's ready to kill me.

"What are you raving about. I know what's going on in every ward. Why don't I hear these things?"

"Why do you ask me? Miss Fairchild, I chart critical patients every day, *every* day, and no one does anything about them. No one questions me about what I write down or if I'm wrong. I write all the charts in English. I know I'm right about these cases. Everybody rides me about the fancy hospital I come from, but we *are* taught when to summon an M.D. And since last week, I've kept carbon copies of my records. Would you like to see them? I can show you a broken arm, a crushed instep, a cracked jaw that has *never* been set, a nonviolent case who doesn't belong there—"

"Do you know that is against the law? Keeping records out of the files? Supposing they were to get into the wrong hands? Into your mother's hands, for example? We have

72

meddlers all the time who don't understand these things. I want you to bring those records to me immediately so they can be destroyed. I ought to dismiss you for breaking the rules. You should know better. If there are any irregularities in the wards, I hear about them. I'll take them up with your supervisor, not with you."

"Miss Fairchild, you were talking about medical ethics. What's going on in that ward has nothing to do with ethics. I'm having a very hard time there. Don't you believe I am telling the truth about what I've been charting?"

"Seward, you're not here to ask questions. You just get those charts or records you have, as I told you. In the meantime, if I see one thing in the newspapers about the activity in this institution, I'll hold you personally responsible. Is that clear?"

"Miss Fairchild, there are articles in the papers right now about one of the doctors. Is that my fault?"

"It might be. It might be."

"That's not fair! I was in WVW only two days when I noticed a bulletin about frontal lobotomies being discontinued, and I didn't have the foggiest idea what it meant. Then I read about that doctor in the newspaper, and I don't even know him. The first two weeks of my affiliation I was in the women's hospital, and I haven't been there since. How could I—?"

"Seward, sit down, don't get so excited. I was merely referring to that in principle."

"But you're ready to throw me out of here on principle!"

"Look, you just get those records, and go back to duty."

"Do you want me to file them with the others?"

"You *are* troublesome, aren't you. *No,* do not file them. Bring them to me. In the meantime, don't forget what I say—no stories in the newspapers, and you can finish your affiliation."

"Yes, ma'am."

Don't rock the boat, Seward. Whatever you do, don't rock the boat. It's not fair, that's all . . . not fair. Well, I don't care. You can have your old records, Fairchild, but I am going to copy them again. Just put a lock on your tenure, Miss Eff, and tighten your blinders. Picking on one lousy student, like I could make or break the place. I just can't fight it. I just can't.

A Day

Neighborhood's the same . . . always been hopeless and dull, until now. Glad to be here today. It is the outside, never felt this way before, outside I like. The home street that I've always run away from I run to happily.

After all the words and thoughts and all things I've privately hoped for, I end being pleased by little things, by life's slender consolations. But maybe not so slender, the film between sanity and madness. If you think you are sane, you believe that you have escaped and only in rare moments do you realize . . .

. . . what is that? Still summer, yet dry leaves. Dry elm leaves, city dry, sounding like the claws of a gawky, long-legged dog sauntering along the sidewalk, blowing after me, making me stop and turn. But only leaves.

The specter of three months, especially these last two weeks, chasing after me until I die. If I could only say I was not there, I was not there . . . some could, quite easily. Patients bad enough, but far worse the people I've worked with . . .

. . . what do I believe? If I spent twenty-two years there, I suppose I might believe something else. Yet . . . I would think that human beings, blessed with reason (perhaps not blessed), seeing the unspeakable suffering . . . I know that they suffer. It's wrong to say that they don't . . . seeing the confused agony of those creatures, would themselves rise to tenderness . . . just once in a while would try

75

more to reach out to them in some helping way . . . to what better use can they possibly put their time and lives while they are here?

. . . I am the world and the center of the world is where I am. I don't know why or anything like that, but I am in the world just the same. In my world, their lives are miserable, mine is good. I have nothing better to do than to try to make their lives less miserable. . . .

. . . but these people who I work for possess no such tenderness or compassion. Why? Is it because of weakness, timidity? Or am I still the way I am because of a timidity and inexperience? No, I am not weak.

Where is my key? Here. Only this time, to unlock to get in, not keep from going out.

"Anybody home?"

No, I guess not. Not expecting me, so I'll surprise them . . . Ed not home from work until later. Mother? Off somewhere. Put my things upstairs . . . no, first in the hall closet, here . . . Lord, this still isn't cleaned out yet. All of father's things, still here. Nobody's gone through them even, dust all over.

For five years they've sat here, and I'm not home long enough to find out. Why did he have two bags? . . . one old, one never . . . and this toilet kit. Maybe I could use it . . . take it upstairs with me. Old bag? What's in it? . . . some of this stuff must date before the war. Should just throw it away. This canvas bundle of, bundle of . . . forgot all about them . . . probes he used in early GC work. Belongs in Smithsonian. Clean it out later. Just junk now. Take the toilet kit upstairs . . . with my bag . . .

. . . these stairs. Wonder if you can oil stairs. Always thought about it, should have tried. Never could get in late after dates without waking up mother. Memorized which ones creaked . . . this one . . . and those two . . . then tried to

76

step over them. Miscounted in the dark, stepped on the wrong ones, sounded like cracking. Might as well have had a gong to hit when I came in. She always wakes up.

. . . Ed's room. Think he could make his bed just once. Mine. Mine at least neat and things put away. No one uses it, and easy to say. Better put these things down, unpack . . . skirt will be a wrinkled mess. Toilet case on the bed, too. Why is it so heavy?

Zip open . . . now, there's an idea: have zippers on all doors at WVW, wouldn't need keys. No, worse, probably, combination locks to open every time we turned around. No wonder this is so heavy . . . good God, I'd have to see it to believe it. Here, I'll put everything on the bed. No, get the spread dirty, so use piece of newspaper. This magazine will do . . . tear a couple of pages out for bigger area. Should have a camera, what is all this?

Two, no, three, four bars of hotel guest-size soap, sample packages of sedatives, three and free, two small envelopes, some nails three large and one two, five larger, a pair of barber shears, a scalpel with cork blade protector, small pair of hemostats. This is ridiculous . . . I wish I could laugh at it. A combination bottle and beer can opener, bottle and bottle cap opener, a blue pencil, a highball stirring rod, a screwdriver, an eye dropper, a flat file and a rat-tail file, another pencil, a thermometer and case, a box of notebook hole reinforcements, a lapel button victory ribbon, another pencil and sheath, a ballpoint pen, one two celluloid rulers, and—what's this?—a prescription powder scale, patent applied for nine-twenty-nine-eighteen eighty-five, a couple of flat ashtrays, a roll of scotch tape and dispenser, two boxes of Digfolin ampules, another box . . . what's in? . . . three syringes and three subcutaneous needles, tincture of Metaphen, some empty vials, two bottles of Coramine oral, I guess.

I can't believe it . . . two paper forks, a collar clasp, a tie clasp, a key ring, a can opener, a styptic pencil and glass tube, a signature stamp pad and stamp (never saw one so small), a tube of Calmitol ointment, some hyperacidity tablets, a light bulb chain, two vials of liquid salt solution, two wooden martini forks, a large paper clip, a belt key holder, a tube of sunburn ointment, a can opener key, another spoon, and a fork and a knife . . . some lint, a razorblade sharpening stone, a rubber band, and . . . and some loose tobacco. Empty that in the basket there . . . look at all this stuff. Why? Why?

Someone coming in downstairs. It's . . . yes, it's Ed.

"Ed, that you?"

No answer. Footsteps on the stairs.

"Well, I didn't know you were coming home. When did you get in? What's all this . . . starting a hobby?"

"No, silly. Just going over the estate of your father and mine. Happened to see it in the hall closet."

"Oh, yes, I just never got around to throwing all that stuff away."

"I'll save you the trouble. But first take a look at all this junk."

Looks. Keeps looking. Says nothing. Well, say something. No, walk away. Well, into the basket . . . he watches me as though I were throwing Father's life away.

"Ed?"

"Yes?"

"Where's Mother?"

"She's spending the weekend with Jessie Davis . . . didn't know you were coming home."

"No, I decided at the last minute. But I don't understand."

"Betty, don't you know what day this is? It's Dad's birthday. Same as Adolf Hitler's."

"Some distinction."

"You know how mother just mills around this place . . . doesn't know what to do with herself. Everything she looks at reminds her of something. I can't do a thing with her. So I suggested it."

"Shall I fix some supper?"

"It'd be great if you would. I'm not going anywhere tonight. Nice to have you home for a change . . . haven't talked to you in ages. How come you came home . . . decided to give up the nursing racket?"

"That's not funny. I'll tell you later. Right now, I want to jump into a tub."

"Every once in a while I come across something—like that toilet case now—just little things, and I realize I never knew Father at all . . . reading little scraps of paper tucked into his notes. I am always finding them, little quotes, bits of private thoughts . . . like the one I found in an old dermatology book. Here, I have it in my purse . . . I'll get it.

"Here it is. Remember he used to read those Chinese proverbs in the newspaper years ago? Here are a few in his handwriting. 'An ounce of oil is worth a ton of powder.' 'A man can be flattered into jumping off a house.' Things like that . . . as if he were off on the moon with nobody to share them."

"Yes, I know, Betty. It's lucky we all have bodies and heads and faces. Otherwise, we'd never recognize each other."

"Eh? Oh, yes. Well, why is that?"

"Why? Because we're all fools for so long that by the time we realize our condition, it's too late to make up for it."

Good thing my own brother has a face and a body.

"Ed, I never could understand how it was possible for

him to have so many friends whom we didn't know existed. One of those nights at the funereal parlor, I was standing near the door reading the visitors' book and a man came up and introduced himself. He looked like a gangster. Said he went to Father several years before and asked him to cure him. He had syphilis or I don't know what—I don't know why he told me all this—and father treated him for months. When he was well, he went to father's office and gave him a big envelope with money in it as a gift."

"You never told me this."

"I know it. Anyway, Father refused to take it and told him if he kept insisting he could get the hell out of the office."

"Sounds just like him."

"Yes, I suppose. He said he was forever indebted to him and would have given him anything . . . finally had something to live for. So a year or two later, he got married and wanted Father to come to the wedding supper . . . big blow-out . . . whole roasted lamb and so forth . . . Greek, maybe, or Armenian . . . he had to go over and drag him out of his office one night. Told him he wouldn't leave without him. So Father went and I guess had a terrific time. He said he brightened up like he had never seen him before . . . was embarrassed they were so good to him. And do you know he never told Mother or anyone. I'm surprised not to Mother. Just went drifting along his own way . . ."

"You know what I'd like to do, Betty? I'm no different from anyone else who plays the jackass while his parents are still alive. I'd like to talk to Dad once more. Just for a moment . . . once more. I've been thinking a lot about him, and it almost breaks me up when I do. I'd like just to shake his hand, to apologize for all the times I thought he was a horses's ass, a social misfit, for all the times I thought he was an incorrigible bastard.

"You know, I've never told you this before, since this is confession night, he once said to me, in that sneering way of his, which I always refused to understand, he said that sociability was the cheapest thing in the world. And you know what I said? I could kill myself for it now. I said, 'And you don't even have that.' So what I'd like to say is, 'Here, please shake my hand—' No, that's not what I'd say. What I'd say is, 'Can I shake your hand? Christ, how did you ever keep from killing me? How did you ever refrain from knocking my head off?' Just that.

"If I could say that, I wouldn't care about anything else. And I think it all the time, every second of my life. If he only knew it. I hope he does.

"God, you know, it's funny, he used to infuriate me with his offhand answers. Now I see that they were so goddamn astute, I could never have understood until he died. I remember, one of the very first medical questions I ever asked him. I was just a dumb punk then. We were walking along the street after dinner, Thanksgiving night, walking off dinner, which he liked to do, and I asked him, 'What's the difference between high blood pressure and low blood pressure? Which was worse to have?' Kind of a dumb question, but I didn't know anything then. And he said, 'Well, with high blood pressure, something's got to give.'

"I didn't say a word the rest of the time we were walking, and what I really wanted to say was, 'Look, don't give me just another smart-aleck answer. Why can't you, just for once, give me a good, solid, professional-sounding answer? Christ, professional-sounding answer. Professional to me then was a solicitous bedside manner, or a bright, house-beautiful type of waiting room, neither of which he had one iota of. And all along he just wanted me to think for myself. He was right; I shouldn't have asked him every

81

half-witted question that came into my head. How am I ever going to straighten something like that out?

"Oh, yes, a bright young student, but pretty stupid, just the same. I remember before you were born, . . . yes, it probably was, because I was very small . . . Aunt Agatha had been sick on and off for months. Agatha told me years later. That was years before anyone had made much progress with TB. And she had been to three or four MDs who were no help at all. So one day she was out for a visit, and very casually, he suggested he listen to her chest. You know, she never thought much of him as a doctor, but the real reason was that he never had too much time for her inane conversation, and unfortunately he let her know that he didn't.

"So after a few objections, she took off her blouse, and he dragged out that old stethoscope, that old one. You'd think that he couldn't hear a bell in a barrel with it. And he listened for a couple of minutes, then said, 'there's only one thing wrong with you. You've got TB.' Well, he might have given her a heart attack with the news, of course, but he hit the nail on the head. That was exactly what was wrong with her, and in a few weeks, she went to a sanitorium. He probably saved her life. But somehow, she never forgave him.

"But there's one thing. I still have a mental image of him that I just can't get rid of. And I've never told you this before, either. It's all part of this whole deal that I just wish I had been able to straighten out before, just so's he'd know that I wasn't planets away. Remember when you were still in school and I was finishing up? I was going with that odd little girl from Peru, and I was going through town on the way to see her. So I stopped off and saw him at his office, and we had some coffee together, and he went with me to the bus depot. I didn't want him to go with me. I hate good-

82

byes to begin with, but more than that, I was ashamed to be seen with him. Can you imagine that? How's that for being a stupid materialistic bastard? You know how he was; he never bought more than one suit at a time, which mother tried frantically to keep pressed—just didn't give a god-damn, I guess, no matter how much I needled him about it.

"I was a lousy conformist. And his hat always looked like the 'before' in a clothing ad. If I was in a particularly sarcastic mood, I'd say something like, 'I'm sorry that you couldn't get that hat off before the hand grenade went off in it. . . .' Whenever I mentioned clothes to him, he always made the same comment: 'To be well-dressed, you should-n't be noticed.' To which I always had some sophomoric comeback, like, 'In that case, you'd either be invisible or ready for Ringling Brothers . . . I don't know which.'

"And that day it was colder than usual . . . January, I guess, so instead of wearing his overcoat, which mother bought for him because he wouldn't go to store, he wore a flimsy topcoat that was good only for Mexican winters, some rag that he should have thrown away years before.

"Well, we stopped in some grease pit for another cup of coffee, which I didn't like, and said so, and it couldn't have made less difference. And then we walked on again to the bus station. I got on the bus, and it pulled out and went around the block before it headed north. He apparently walked around the other way to see if he could see me once again.

"As the bus started north finally, I saw him, standing on the sidewalk next to a parking lot. There wasn't another person around anywhere. You could tell it was cold out be-cause he had his coat collar turned up and the wind whipped against his skinny legs. He had on his perpetual scowl, underneath that impossible hat, and he looked hard at the bus to see if he could see me. Well, stupid jerk that I was, I refused to wave . . . everyone in the bus would know that I would be waving to him, and that he was probably my father; there wasn't anyone else around, so I would have to be waving to him.

"He saw me, I know, and he took his hand away from his collar for an instant and started to wave, then hesitated. I didn't even turn my head. Well, no, finally I did, but by that time, he had started to walk the other way, leaning into the wind, careening his unsure way, like he was on a loose tightrope or something.

"I don't know what happened inside my bird brain, but all of a sudden, I realized what I had done. And suddenly, I realized somehow that he was really sick. All I could think of the whole trip was that wisp of a man bucking the wind or being carried away by it and what an insufferable sonofabitch I was. I just fell apart. I couldn't help myself.

"And I remember there was a Negro woman sitting next to me, and she asked me if something was wrong. I didn't even answer her at first, and when I did, I said, 'everything,' which naturally didn't make any sense. I had done my very best to alienate him. He needed me but would never say so. If I had had any character, I would have gotten off that rotten bus and spent the whole weekend with him. But I had no character.

"The woman next to me was a madame in a Negro whorehouse, I found out, catering to white trade by the way, and we got talking, about her business mostly, because I was snooping, about the police protection she kicked in for and her boyfriends, and it took my mind off things. But I was lousy company the whole weekend. That picture kept coming back to me.

"Just once, just once, I'd like to shake his hand. And you know, that was the last time I ever saw him in street clothes, because he went into the hospital two weeks later, and when I saw him after that, he was in pajamas."

He looks away from me, and I'll wait because I don't mind. Pajamas . . . nothing but pajamas from then on.

"All these years, Ed, we've known each other, you're not the same person I grew up with."

"Only the names are the same to point out the guilty."

"No, seriously, Ed, we've never talked about father. I didn't know you felt this way."

"You don't, can't, talk about everything. I never knew him, and though I know him now, it couldn't make less difference. That's the hellish thing about living; you never really know anything about anyone."

What is he talking about?

"Well, anyway, as I was saying, Ed, I walked into the dayroom, and, and the atmosphere was more tense than ever before. It was like something had just happened, and I had missed it. All those wrecks were huddled in groups around the room. They weren't milling about or standing like so many tubes of detached silence, isolated from each other. No, it was like they had all suffered some shock in common, something ugly which affected them all in the same way.

"I knew immediately; there had been a real row. I was sure of it. And on one side of the room against the wall was a woman sitting on the floor. She looked like someone had propped her up there. Well, that didn't matter, but her face. Her poor face. Someone had given her a going over. Both her eyes were black, swollen shut. Severe contusions under both eyes, and her nose was twice its normal size.

"I bent down to look at her, and she didn't move. I reached out to touch her, to see if her nose was fractured, and the second I touched her, she let out a scream that scared me half to death. She didn't let up, but kept up a wail. Then they all started, laughing, shrieking.

"But that couldn't have just happened to that woman. It must have been hours before. And do you know, the two attendants didn't even move?

"Then as I looked across the room, I could see into that dreadful excuse for a bathroom, and another patient was lying face down in the floor.

"One of the attendants saw me walk that way and tried to block my path. Well, I really blew up. One of them, I don't know, could have been this Phoebe girl, said something to me about not bothering, that she'd be all right or something. I didn't pay any attention, just pushed her aside.

"That woman lying on the floor had a deep gash in her head and was out cold. I could have sworn one of the attendants did it, but I couldn't prove it. I asked if anyone had called the hospital, and neither of them even answered me. So I went out and slammed the door so hard, it shook the building. There was a second of silence, then the laughing and shrieking started all over again.

"Naturally, *naturally*, neither Fenwick nor Benson was around, so I grabbed the telephone and called for an ambulance. You know, when you call like that, you have to give your name because they're all afraid one of the patients will call or somehow get to a phone.

"I told the operator I was a student and that I couldn't find my supervisor. And do you know, it was nearly an hour before an ambulance got there. I sat in the hall and waited. When it arrived, I left and went back to the dorm. I was sick.

"I tried to find out how that woman was and got nowhere. But word gets around. She never regained consciousness and died two days later. When I heard, I guess I cried like a baby. I never did find out about the one with the broken face, so I don't know what they ever did with her."

"God, that's awful."

"And it's times like this that I wish I could talk to Father."

"You'd think he'd be reassuring? I know what he'd say that it was about time that you realized that people are barely up off all fours."

"That wouldn't be any help."

"It wouldn't, eh? That's what you think now."

"Well, why go on? I could sit here all night and spell out one savage story after another."

"You needn't. I've heard enough."

"I suppose so. I've gone back to my room each night for two weeks and couldn't eat my supper, such as it was. Had to come home this weekend just to get away."

"I'm glad you did. Mother was telling me that you've been telephoning every night."

"Well, something really should be done."

"Why?"

"What do you mean, 'why?' "

"I mean, I mean, there's no sense in doing anything. Just try to forget the whole thing."

"Ed, I don't understand you."

"Look, Betty, you've only got less than one week more. You just can't go on feeling sorry for the whole world."

"Yes, I know. But don't you see, Ed, hundreds of students go through and say that. I've only got 'one week more.' Meanwhile, there are a hundred and fifty human statistics being beaten and starved to death."

"I know, I know. I know all that. This is the twentieth century, rocketry, and going for the moon, but that's all. Otherwise, you're still in the Middle Ages or anything you want to call it. But you, one student, are not going to accomplish a thing."

"You're talking to your sister, Ed. Remember? You're talking to me. Don't be so cynical."

"I'm telling you, that's all. The whole thing is too big. Look, you poor idealist, for years a lot of pretty smart people on all the newspapers in town have had their reporters committed. They've made monkeys out of a few small-time sadists, some of whom have been fired. But what has it accomplished? They've sold a lot of papers, because their business is selling papers. And in a week, a month, it blows over. In the end, who cares? They never get to the right people. And the right people are protecting their jobs. Here you are. There have been a few scandals recently, but nothing has changed."

"Ed, I don't want to argue about it. I'm too tired. If you're so smart, who *are* the right people?"

"How should I know? It's a state-supported institution. How do you get at anyone?"

"Look, I'm positive something can be done. I know I am right about what I see with my own eyes. No one has ever tried to do a real job."

"Betty, that is a loose and foolish generality."

"I mean, the way they run the violent wards, everyone thrown together, the wrong ones there, everything. The trouble has to be at the top."

"Why must it?"

"Why? Because someone hires the lousy help, and they are unsupervised. They run wild. I just told you."

"Now, wait a minute. There are always bound to be a few rotten ones. It's like everywhere else."

"You don't know what you're talking about! Let's take just one thing."

"All right, let's."

"That ward is loaded with incompetent fools and savages. Even the main kitchen, for God's sake. I know what they get paid. You can't get the right help for the measly salaries they pay. Just as a start, they need more money for salaries and food."

"What are you going to do? Examine the books?"

"And why not? Someone should."

"Because it wouldn't prove anything. How do you know if they have enough money. How do you know if they need more? How would you know if you saw the figures. Did you ever see a state or city budget? They're a matter of public record, you know."

"Yes, I know, I know."

"Well, you ought to read one. Look, you're a young girl. Use all the CPAs in town, and some self-righteous state rep on an appropriations committee will make mincemeat of you. It's his business to get money through legislation. These people appropriate millions every year and can prove it. You'll be branded a meddler and a fool. This state is not so bad. Do you know that some states appropriate just enough money to keep their institutions going? I know of one big hospital right near here where the only psychiatrist in residence is the chief medical officer, and there's not another one on the entire staff."

"I don't care about that. Look, Ed, all I know is that a better salary would attract a better class of people. These people know it. You know it. I know it. If they've got it, they could get the right people. It's as simple as that."

"Like hell it's that simple. Supposing they don't want to pay more?"

"I can't believe it."

"Yes, you can. Look, I can't justify what anyone's doing. How would I know, anyway? But think about it. Why doesn't it make sense to concentrate money and attention on patients who can leave sometime? Of course, that ward you've been in is terrible. But those woman will never get out. From one viewpoint, it's like pouring money down a rathole."

"Ed, I'm not arguing that. But I've told you that I've seen women in that hole who don't belong there. It's the nuttiest kind of public morality I can imagine. Everyone pays lip service to one thing and does something else—"

"That's a portrait of the world."

"Even the hopeless ones have needs too, even though psychotic ones. Families surrender their own to WVW, believing that they'll be cared for. Wellingham betrays that confidence. It's open defiance of public faith, it makes me sick."

"What time is it?"

"Nearly midnight. I've got to get to bed."

"Uh-huh, so do I. Betty, why do I always have to be the perennial crepe hanger? The lesson is being spelled out for you, and you won't even read it. This thing's bugging you, yet you haven't got a reason in the world to expect any help. The only thing you can do is to do what you're doing. What more can you ask of yourself? Face it, don't get thrown out on your ear."

"Two rotten weeks that have filled me with terror and disgust for the whole human race—"

"It takes some people a whole lifetime to find that out. You're lucky."

"More of your cynicism. I've got a week to go. I don't know if I'll make it. There must be someone who'll listen to me. I'd really feel like I've accomplished something, at least."

"Betty, Betty, Betty, why be a martyr to a hopeless cause? You've simply got to get this thing in focus. For each one like you who seems to believe in humanity, there are countless thousands who make it perfectly clear every day of their lives that they don't give a goddamn about anything. Nothing but lip service. Most people who insist that they believe in the human race give me a pain in the behind. You see the evidence every day—charity balls, professionally organized funds, seminars for old ladies on mental health—seminars, for chrissake! . . . a common variety of fair-weather compassion strictly compatible with their own time and self-interests. Don't give them a tough problem.

"How could you help but notice? We're all going to the moon, but we can't keep water out of our basements or cut down juvenile delinquency or accept integration in a rapidly changing world or solve a hundred other earth-bound problems. And do you know why? Because going to the moon is easier.

"You'll be a troublemaker for ever bringing this thing up. People will deem it their Christian duty to straighten you out, but they won't help. If you're not with them, you're against them, and they'll slap you down, just a little, to show you the way. And 'the way' is conformity to the world's way, the way of sodden indifference. If you're not that 'way,' then you are intolerant. This is our society's peculiar notion of tolerance."

"No, it's not true—"

"Oh, it is so. Think of how many Christeres there are in the world. You've got to see things their way. Hell, it's like a lay preacher in the Bible belt exhorting the flock to give up smoking and drinking on Sunday, then foreclosing a mortgage on Monday—"

"No, it's not true. You are off on one of your insufferable, cynical tangents. My profession wouldn't even exist if it weren't for the kind of people you say don't exist. I meet selfless, interested people every day."

"You may, but is the situation any better now than it ever was?"

"Of course it is. Now about all the medical advancements?"

"Medical advancements. Now, that's another thing. Have you noticed lately how your doctor's relationship with his patients has advanced. When was the last time you made an appointment with a doctor? Oh, that's right, you can see one anytime you please. But I can't. There's a little piece of standard equipment an MD should have when he starts out, a plaque that reads, 'Plan Your Sickness.' He can hang it on his door just to let everyone know he's gone high class. Or he could put up a schedule, 'broken leg, earaches, split-open heads by appointment only; cuts and bruises two weeks in advance.' "

"Oh, come on, Ed."

"Or 'Warning! Don't become deathly ill on Wednesdays, Saturdays, Sundays, or in the morning. Pneumonia and other grave illnesses during office hours only.' And if he wanted to go real class, 'Written application for house calls to be countersigned by a notary public.' But don't get me off on that subject."

"Yes, spare me that tonight, anyway."

My brother, my brother, what has happened to you? I can't even get moral help from you.

"Betty, what have medical advancements got to do with a drama you've just described. The inhumanity dates back to the Middle Ages?"

"We're arguing, Ed, and I didn't come home for that."

"Yes, that's true, and I'm sorry. But it just seems to me that the sooner you reconcile your hypersensitivity to this ugliness, the better off you'll be. And you won't get an ulcer.

"People are unforgivable. I love them, and I'll champion the cause of an individual anytime, anywhere, but people are still irrevocably and totally unforgivable. Otherwise, in your own case, you wouldn't be seeking the emotional refuge of your own home, such as it is, from that madhouse. Life is a series of madhouses, some more subtly controlled than others, but even more terrifying if you take time to think about them. You just can't spend your life seeking refuge from them all.

"You have only one choice: have enough confidence in yourself to believe that what you are doing is the best you can do and all you can do. If it seems to make no ripple on the water of life's indifference, you still don't lose. But you have to believe that you don't lose."

A Day

Should have gotten back earlier last night . . . really need more sleep. In spite of all our words, weekend went too fast. Peaceful to be home, at least, away from the unkindnesses of . . . should have gotten started earlier this morning. Now, a little late. First time.

That's strange, Wallace rushing up walk . . . no, going into WVW. At this hour? Wonder if he caught hell for that big fight last week? Why should he, though? Better follow.

He's going into dayroom. Haven't seen him go in there for several days. What's he in such a hurry about? Don't know how he can put up with the filth. Paid to keep his mouth shut? Can't be. What is he paid, I wonder?

Follow him in.

Key here.

Shut click.

Yes, take a *good* look around. Says nothing. Walking into bathroom. Bathroom. Filthy sty. Stops at door. Hands on hips. What? Beckoning attendant.

"Miss Steward, will you come here, please?"

Something wrong? More wrong than everything is?

"Miss Seward, I want you to look at this. Why wasn't I informed of this?"

"Doctor, I just came on duty this minute—"

What are you talking about? Oh . . . oh, my God . . . Fleming girl . . . lying on the floor, gown half-torn off. Head in the toilet bowl. I can hardly look . . . feel like throwing up. Head in the bowl. Water all over her. Stinks. Putrid gagging smell.

"Have you been observing this patient, Miss Seward?"

"Why, yes, Doctor. I talked to you last week about her."

"I don't remember that."

What do you mean, you don't remember?

"Don't you remember? I stopped you in the outside hall, Doctor, and—"

"Miss Seward, people stop me all day long. How am I supposed to remember every conversation day after day?"

"Yes, sir." Dirty liar.

"Have you been observing this patient—here, help me lift her onto a chair."

A chair? What chair?

"Attendant, get me a chair."

Phoebe again, hurrying across the room, shoves that woman onto the floor. Woman falls, lays there, stays there. Let's play statue, I'll go first. Phoebe bumps everything getting over here. Knocks over two more women. They fall over each other. One slaps the other like it was her fault. Upset the whole room before we're through.

"Here, that's it, put her on it. Have you been observing her, Miss Seward?"

"Yes, Doctor, I have."

"Have you been charting her behavior?"

"Every day I've made some entry. So has everyone else."

"Will you get her chart. I'll be out in the hall."

Not that you don't believe me. That's right, leave her on the chair, only to fall off again. Suddenly you get super efficient. Don't worry, I'll get it.

Key.

Click open, open, shut click.

Every student on duty has put something down. Must

be ten pages added in the last week. You want to make a lesson out of this, we can. Fenwick's door.

Key in.

Click, open, open, shut click.

Gee, aitch, dee, ee, here eff, Fleming. Oh, no, this is not possible . . . nothing but blank pages . . . maybe misfiled. Hmm, not here, nor here. Now, where?

. . . wonder if that was a loaded question? Why were you so persistent? No, it's not possible. Step to door.

Click open, open.

"Dr. Wallace, will you come in here, please?"

Back to file. Maybe in the wrong drawer. Footsteps.

"What is it, Miss Seward?"

"Doctor, here is the chart, but at least ten pages of entries are missing. Not only mine, but other students' observations. I don't know where they could be, unless they were misfiled."

What I really mean is 'thrown away.'

"Look, Miss Seward, things like charts are *not* lost around here."

"Doctor, I don't do the filing."

"Why don't you?"

"Why don't I? Because I am not supposed to."

Stop smiling like a silly ass. You know there have been entries every day . . . if you don't, you haven't looked for at least a week.

"Let's start keeping an *accurate* record, shall we?"

Turns, walks right out of the room. Where's he going? Out of the building? Why not back to the day room? What's going on around here, anyway? Must think I'm stupid or something. Knows damned well there have been entries. Meantime, the Fleming girl will have her head back in the toilet bowl before we know it . . . what's he going to do about her? Can't be a conspiracy just against me. Impossible. Too many people in and out of here every day. But that could have been a trap for me. Maybe Fairchild in on this . . . good thing I didn't volunteer my carbon copies, then I'd really be in a mess and get thrown out. No, I'll just take the rap for this if there's going to be one . . .

. . . except that it seems too incredible, Fenwick could possibly spend her time covering up for mistakes . . . tears records off charts. Nice way to protect against law suits by families. No, I can't believe it . . . still . . . Wallace doesn't make regular rounds. Neither does his relief. No one does. Just for EST and emergency . . . I never see any of these characters. No daily entries by MDs on charts . . . just blame students, if necessary, for lack of entries . . .

. . . just can't stand here. What's Fleming scheduled for . . . not hydro, let's see, no, not pheno. Nothing. Scheduled to rot with the rest. Must do something . . . no medications lying around here, for sure. Fenwick, even Benson, keeps everything locked up like a vault. If I could sneak some phenobarbital out of pheno downstairs . . . no, I don't dare do that . . . one of Fenwick's informers would really fix me. Maybe I could talk to her a little bit . . . no, then they'll all be on my neck. Could comb her hair. I just don't know. Better go see how she is . . . and, oh, yes, make an entry on this chart right now. But first, I'd better go in there.

Where are . . . here they are, keys.

Click open, open, shut click.

A Day

While I have the chance . . . no one around yet . . . I'll check my naked old lady, see if she's making any progress. Progress, that's a laugh . . . well, getting used to a routine. Got to be persistent. She'll fall into her old way so easily. Who'll do it when I am gone? Why do I want to keep clothes on her, anyway? Doesn't make sense, I know. I guess . . . will never never get used to human beings falling to pieces. I'm hopelessly sentimental . . . trying to preserve a little dignity for each, until the end.

But interesting to see if it's possible. Each day she keeps them on a little longer. Yesterday it was . . . how long? . . . about three hours.

Key.

Click open . . .

There she is . . . oops, same old skin. Get a clean uniform. Key. Shut click.

Click open, open . . .

Funny, we start out discovering the world when we're young, and for awhile, we're born over again each day. If we learn anything, we stay born . . . but in the end, if we're unlucky, we start being born again, all over again, each day. Which sounds like around . . . big cheer for the three blind mice.

Shut click.

This should do. No buttons, ties in the back.

Key again.

Click open, open, shut click.

Where is she now? Oh, there, walking to the window . . . that's just fine. Standing near the radiator. Thank goodness there's no heat up, this place would smell worse than it does already. Go over. Oh, oh, that big one, the long hair . . . don't even give them haircuts in here . . . gives naked old lady a shove, she falls crack against the radiator . . . falls down on one knee. Better take a chance and get in the middle of that . . .

. . . pick her up . . . still cowering . . . doesn't know me today.

"Look what I have for you, a nice new dress."

Looks at me finally, doesn't smile, holds out arms . . .

"There . . . isn't that nice? A new dress for you. That's it, turn around. No, turn this way." Now tie in back. She pulls on it, but no buttons to pull off. Stands looking down at herself, as usual. Doesn't move. We'll see how long that lasts. I'll check at lunch.

Quite a few naked today. Could never keep them all dressed . . . no help from Phoebe or Nancy . . . they just sit there, snickering as always. Well, got to go.

Key here.

Click open, open, shut click.

Almost forgot, EST schedules for today . . . let's see, extra students scheduled for duty. Haven't witnessed one since Fulton. Where am I listed? One, two . . . five, six. I see . . . Seward, standby. Just as well, I can learn today. Graduate on list also. No name . . . just word. Better get started taking temps. Patient roster, where is it? Here. Between ten and twelve, EST. Two hours for . . . for, how many? Two, four, six . . . eighteen, twenty-four and ten and six. Heaven's sake, forty patients. In two hours? Better check names, get numbers, too. Note here . . . remove patients from "up" roster if running temperature . . . must remember. Make notations on chart if not up . . .

. . . wonder why EST not given in phenobarb downstairs? Have to go to ward. Patients must be used to what's in store when they're kept away from dayroom. How're they kept peaceful? . . . must watch when others given treatment, know they're going to get it, too. Have to be oblivious to the world, to stand by not knowing that you're next . . . how can forty ESTs be given in one morning? . . .

. . . here comes Wallace, all sweetness and light . . . must have the hide of a hippo . . . like nothing was wrong, looks right through me. No, sir, don't worry, I won't forget yesterday, you rat. Oh, oh, here comes Fenwick, carrying machine and, and Cookie. The others coming, too, two, three, four, must be new. Haven't seen them before in the dorm. Nice way to start your affiliations, in women's violent.

"Morning, Cookie, didn't know you were on this morning. Would have walked over here with you."

No one else speaking . . . everyone quiet and obedient. They'll learn.

"Good morning, Betty, back to the grind. Keep asking myself, 'what am I doing here?' Just get here?"

"A few minutes ago."

Yes, what am I doing here? Lucky don't have to say that all the time. Never know what life brings to you. Outside today, in here tomorrow. Terrible, terrible. By that time, doesn't make any difference, though.

"What's Wallace doing here so early?"

Fenwick going into her office. Wallace follows.

"I don't know. Oh, he's leaving again. Heard him say something about temperatures not being taken yet."

"What's the matter with him? He knows better than that. I just came on duty. They couldn't possibly be charted

100

yet. Maybe he has to catch a bus to the track . . . or to the garage."

"Well, I suppose we might as well get at it. Let's go upstairs."

"Okay. Worked with EST before?"

"A couple of times. I'll tell you about it."

Everyone's all right, I guess . . . no temp . . . no, except this one . . . she even looks like she has one. Let's see, hundred and . . . hundred and two. Have to check this one off . . . should get the chart. Wonder if she had any yesterday. No time to go downstairs now . . .

"Cookie, will you come here a minute." She's . . . she's a mess . . . mouth dry . . . pulse? "Let me have your hand . . . no, I won't hurt you . . . that's a girl." Pulse going a mile a minute.

"What's the matter?"

"Feel her pulse . . . thermometer's a hundred and two and two-tenths."

"She's not ready today. Maybe we can sponge her a little. I'll get a couple of the others. Say, will you come here a minute?"

"Can I help?"

"Yes. What's your name?"

"Lucy."

"Lucy, take that girl with you. Get some towels and cool water. We want to sponge her, maybe bring down her temperature. Tell you what. You get her chart, I'll get the towels. Be right back, Betty."

. . . funny I didn't notice her when I first came in here . . . doesn't even move, so drowsy.

"That's all right, honey, we'll take care of you. You'll be all right."

You'll probably never be all right, but you won't know

the difference. How do these things slip by these fool attendants. She's probably been feverish all night . . .

"Here are some towels, Betty. A roll of cotton, we can wash her face. The other girl's bringing a basin. Here's Lucy with the chart. How about it, Lucy?"

"No temperature charted yesterday, but hundred and one the day before yesterday."

"Wasn't anything done about it?"

"No, Betty, nothing else here. Want to see it?"

"Yes, please."

Let's see. G. Brandwon. Age forty-five. Been here six months. Involutional melancholic, EST last week. Another . . . another two weeks ago. Today's not her day, though . . .

. . . there goes Fenwick by door, finally. Wallace behind her . . . carrying a folding chair. Folding chair? Two students bringing in the machine . . . what do they call it? Small box, two handles, long wire trailing. All going into that side room. Follow. Other student setting up folding stand for stretcher. So that's why a stretcher in every ward. This room couldn't be more bare. One lousy table, no chairs . . . I see, Wallace bring his own, sits at table. Make yourself comfortable, doctor, just like playing house, isn't it? Fenwick setting up some jars on table, sterile gauze, look like rolled up compresses, jar of what looks like Vaseline. Oh, yes, lubricating jelly. What's that? Looks like bag of flour, no, sand.

"Miss Fenwick, will you have them get the first one?"

"Yes, Doctor. Girls, start with C, bring in the first patient. Better four of you go. Miss Koch, ask one of the attendants to bring up some more straps from storage. I notice that a number of them are missing in B and D. Come back immediately, we'll probably need you."

"Hall storage?"

"No phenobarb. Now, hurry. Girls, you had better wait until she comes back."

Why go down two flights? There's a cabinet up here. Twenty-one years in this place and still doesn't know where things are. Maybe she does. Ten o'clock now . . . counted just about forty patients. I think it would take all day to get through. We can't stay up here that long . . . I've got a thousand things to do. Let's see, once a week for EST, been going on for months . . . must be a lot of repeats. Do they remember? No, they don't . . . wonder if some do. Have a lot more trouble, I imagine, if they did. Look at Wallace, look at him. Cleaning his nails, staring into space . . . hardly moved a muscle since he's been in that chair. What's he need a chair for? I'd like one, too.

The silence is ear-splitting. Fenwick, absorbed in thought, as if turned to stone . . . like everyone around her. We've all turned to stone. Fenwick, looks at me, looks away . . . must be horrible, living a life with a house full of specters. This is the world, this is the world . . . what is it Ed says, heard him so many times at home, badgering us all, so you think this is the world, we live our little insular existences, et cetera, et cetera, or something like that . . . we go our own sweet way and nothing touches us.

Nothing touches us . . . what was he talking about? If you see the world as everyone else sees it, you don't see it at all. Well, if this is the world that I see, I don't want it, anyway . . . I don't want it. Remember that letter he wrote me from college. A man is born, he suffers, and he dies. Must have read that somewhere. Why should he say that? No right to . . . unless this is the world. Almost believe him when I look around.

Fenwick *still* still standing there . . . this is ridiculous . . . like taking time away from us, until Cookie comes back upstairs. Want so much to believe there's some way during

103

this moment I am here to help these women . . . suffering beyond all the corny ideas of expression . . . that's what we learn, corny ideas. Like formulas in a language we never learned. But they must want to see God, too, and know somehow that he is watching over them. All expression lost . . . crushed out of them by the world . . . crushed into silence . . .

. . . here comes Cookie. Fenwick motioning for the girls to go . . . errand of horror. Come along, lady, we have a big surprise for you. In five years . . . in five minutes, you'll never know the difference . . .

. . . here they come with her already. She doesn't want to, doesn't have the physical strength to resist. Everyone pulling her, dragging. She's terror-stricken. Wallace doesn't even look up. Picking her up, putting her on the stretcher. No restraints? All five holding her.

Fenwick picks up bag from table, sandbag, puts it under her back. Struggling, struggling. Starting to scream, dreadful animals sounds. Fenwick grabbing gauze compress from jar, rolls tightly, shoves it into woman's mouth. Ooh, she's rough . . . woman tries to spit it out. Fenwick pushes it back in, stuffs it in. Grabs rubberband attached to wire, electrodes on either side. Tongue depressor into jelly. She rubs it on electrodes. Rubberband onto woman's head, electrodes at temples . . .

"Seward, don't stand there gaping, hold her head while I straighten the band."

Hold head, lubricating jelly all over her head, what a mess.

"This right, Cookie?"

"Yes, now hold her shoulders."

Wallace still hasn't moved. What's he here for? Official sanction, I suppose.

"Okay, Doctor."

Oh, I see . . . he pushes button. Adjusts dial, pushes . . . now. Bow. Now . . .

. . . my God, does she jump! Convulsions . . . never saw such violent convulsions. No wonder we don't use restraints . . . she'd dislocate her back or a leg. Is that all? No, another charge, another backbreaking jolt . . . convulsions again, again!

"All right, next one."

He speaks he moves. Stamp of approval.

. . . students wheeling her back. Go along. One taking restraints along. Others hold her on . . . convulsions would throw her off. Get my keys out.

Here.

Click open, open, shut click.

Across room. Placing her in bed, tying her down, legs and arms . . . wrists . . . full restraints. Better help get the next one . . . there she is, cowering on the floor, won't look at us. Like it'd make us disappear. How come more don't pass out from fright? Think they'd have a coronary . . . but, no, condemned to good health . . . hanging on to physical life. How?

. . . never mind, two have her already . . . not resisting.

"Cookie, why the mouth gag? She could hardly breathe."

"If we don't put one in, she'll grind her teeth and loosen them. Fenwick's supposed to put it behind the front teeth. Haven't you noticed that some have their front teeth missing? If the gag isn't put in right, they'll grind them loose . . . eventually lose them. They don't remember getting an EST and complain, not knowing why their teeth are falling out. Better get back."

Key again.

Click open, open, shut click.

Back to ugly room. Dragging reluctant patient along corridor, through doorway . . .

"Don't be so goddamn slow, you people . . . throw her on the stretcher. Do you think we've got all day?"

Yes, throw her up there, like a bag of garbage. Sandbag again, under back. Everyone holding her down. Jelly on electrodes, band around head, Fenwick reaching for new compress, at least takes a fresh—why so sanitary all of sudden?—it's hard to hold her head down. Steady. Steady. Gauze in mouth. In mouth. Not far enough, not in . . .

"Miss Fenwick . . ."

"All right, Doctor."

Fenwick careless . . . not in far enough. One charge, Wallace just sits there pushing button . . . she stiffens . . . sickening, she's squirming, one agonizing convulsion . . . she relaxes, stiffens again . . . good thing we're holding her down. Wallace presses button again. Now he's watching. About time.

That's enough. Enough! What's the matter with that gauze, it's not in far enough.

"Miss Fenwick . . . !"

"Will you shut up, Seward! Once again, Doctor?"

No, not again. No, no.

"Hold on to her, once more."

Wallace presses again. Christ, what's happening to her? . . . why, she's dislocated her jaw! Badly . . . blood trickling out of her mouth . . . Wallace jumps up, leans over her . . . pulls her chin forward, forward . . . it's back . . . I think I'm going to faint. No, I mustn't. Mustn't. She's in agony. Fenwick wiping her face. Still have to hold her on the stretcher. Wallace motioning her away . . . like a judgment . . . no sedation . . . just suffer through with impossible courage . . .

Off one stretcher, onto another, back to the ward. Walking the last mile, up and back, thirty-eighth time. Feel like an executioner who didn't quite make the grade. Back to the ward . . .

"Got a key, Betty?"

"Yes, here, I've got it."

Click open, open . . . in the goes.

Wait.

Finally. Shut, click.

And close the incinerator door.

Back to ward. What are they waiting for?

"Well, Seward, where's the last one?"

"That *is* the last one, Miss Fenwick."

"What do you mean, 'last one'? That's only thirty-eight."

"Oh, she's running a temperature, hundred and two . . . for more than twenty-four hours—"

"Miss, what is your name?"

"Koch, Doctor."

"Is she scheduled for today?"

"Yes, she is, Doctor, but I thought she was supposed to be rescheduled if she had a temperature."

"No, no, if this is her scheduled day, we'll have to go through with it."

"Seward, you and Koch bring her here."

"Yes, ma'am. Come on, Cookie."

Back to the ward again.

Key here.

Click open, open, shut click.

"What can we do, Cookie?"

"How should I know? Just be glad she's not your own family. Help me get her up. We'll walk her back."

But she is my family . . . how can I express it?

"That's the trouble, Cookie, she is my family."

"Oh, Betty, this is no time to be philosophical. Here, take hold of her arm."

"I've got her. That's it. What else can anyone?"

"Nothing, just nothing."

"Hold her, Cookie, while I unlock the door."

Click open, open . . .

"Got her. That's it. Now, wait a second."

. . . shut click.

"Lord, she's heavy. Just so much dead weight."

"Yes, one way or the other."

On the stretcher.

Sandbag again, under back. Fenwick looking at her, hesitates. Hesitates.

Looks at Wallace, keeps looking, but he doesn't bat an eye.

Jelly on electrodes, band around head, Fenwick finally reaching for gauze compress, keeps looking at her, puts it in her mouth. Everyone silent. This is terrible. Should all be wearing black masks. No good. Can't hide the shame of it.

Wallace waiting unperturbed . . . gauze well in her mouth. Everyone holding her down. Wallace presses button. Now.

What? What's happening? Can't hold her down . . . down! She's going completely haywire? Writhing in horrible agony. My God, my God, like a mad dog . . . wriggling, gagging, saliva bubbling all over her mouth . . . she's not human . . . almost jerks off table . . . Wallace still not helping . . . completing calm. Unmoving. No, Wallace, this is not your family . . . she's some creature from the moon . . . your move, Doctor.

"Take her off the table . . . into the ward, quickly, heavy restraints."

Even Fenwick looks surprised.

"But, Doctor, shouldn't I call the hospital . . . take her over there?"

"No, she'll be all right. Restraints will do the trick."

Yes, Doctor, an iron maiden would help, too.

Back to the ward. She's still frothing at the mouth. More convulsions. Look. Look. Can't take eyes off her. A wreck. Total physical and mental wreck. But still alive. How? Why?

"Got your key, Betty?"

"Yes, here."

Click open, open, shut click.

Tying her down. Better cover her well. That's it. Cookie and other girl, pale as waxpaper, sponging her again. She's quieting a little. Live through it all?

Want to get out of here. Out. Out.

My key . . . where is? Here.

Click open, open . . .

"Coming, Cookie?"

"Think I'll stick around for a few minutes. I want watch her for a little while."

"All right. Not me."

. . . shut, click.

Corridor.

No one here, not a soul. As if it all never happened . . . never, never . . .

A Day

Never so thankful in my life to get out of any place . . . miserable forty-five minutes for lunch which I can't eat. Couldn't gag anything down. Little difference it'll make. Didn't miss anything, anyway.

Thirty-nine patients in one morning, *one* morning . . . playing some horrible, nauseous little game with thirty-nine frantic souls, all begging for mercy until you almost believe they know what they're saying, like a fantastic joke on the entire human race. How could he sit there unmoved and unmoving, I'll never know. What must one be made of to persist? Thirty-nine sets of restraints. Thirty-nine females guilty of still being alive . . . and being guilty, condemned to being kept alive. Great Christian tradition and a fear of lawsuits. But no fear of lawsuits if licensed to experiment with human life . . .

. . . yes, practice, practice. It's one thing to practice doing it right. But to practice doing it wrong? Why in God's name are we giving them EST? Every other week. All week, they get kicked around and fed unspeakable slop because it's not supposed to matter in all their hopelessness . . . and the in-between weeks they get practiced with EST, in spite of their hopelessness. We chart them day-in, day-out, like we needed the handwriting practice. No one reads what we struggle with, and no one believes us when we do show them the charts; but it's EST just the same . . .

110

. . . like using two different scripts for the same play and asking us to believe the plot . . .

. . . they can't spare an MD to make regular rounds, but they can waste his time fifty-two times a year giving EST to those they tell us can't be helped with anything . . .

Fenwick told me to read my orientation and I read it. And that woman should have been rescheduled . . . is this the science I have dedicated myself to? How can I live with this filthy nonsense?

Easy enough to walk out of there when my time is up . . . will walk out for good in just a few days . . . but walk to the edge of the world, and off, I suppose, and still can't walk away from everything . . .

. . . nice to have a plug in your head somewhere so you could pull it out and let the wind blow through. Just to blow away forever things seen and heard. Or better yet, to pull from your brain the adhesions of bad memories. Slam them down on a table and say something like, here, this is what in my human shame I have seen and know, and I want you, you, and you to know it by sight and feeling, and don't forget the smell. This is the way it is, and at last I can tell you . . .

Remember in school used to watch the track meets, and hurdlers on the inside lane . . . would start behind the others to make the race even. But suppose . . . how did I ever think of this? . . . suppose they all started at the same place? And some wore track shoes and others had their legs tied together. And then the lanes were all different . . . strewn with broken glass and knee-deep banana custard and crazier things, like barbed wire, quicksand, pouring rain, maybe scrap iron, moon gravity, or velvet and I don't know what else. Then no runner knew what the others had, but thought that everyone had the same . . .

. . . what is really so different about this?

And each thinks he hears the same starting gun, and off he goes.

. . . what is really so different about this?

But I can't pull whatever it is out of my head or out of my sight or memory, a string of something, and put it down in front of the world. You're a fool, Seward, for being so sentimental . . .

. . . you're a fool, fool, but I can't help it. No one starts at the same place in life, and some don't survive on the way . . . they stop bouncing back, can't take every blow . . . because they stop being human beings, we're not to treat them like human beings. You fool, Seward, try presenting your little argument to your profession and they'll shut you off and won't listen, or they'll tell you that they're trying, they're trying . . . some nice little speech you'll get . . . and a thicket to the next psychiatrist . . . just to show me the way, as Ed says. They'll say that it doesn't make any difference to those poor women, and maybe we're actually helping some . . . maybe we are, but they can't take away what I see with my own eyes . . .

. . . life among the wreckage, even just a little life, my life . . . physical and mental wreckage, we've helped get them that way, hanging hysterically onto life for a reason that no one can give them or me or anyone . . . and soon I can't tell right from wrong. Then *I* will need a psychiatrist . . . it's catching.

A Day

Back to two stories of no principles, for the last time. The last time. After everything that's happened, I dread to leave in a way . . . always dread leaving if job is undone. But how could I do the whole job alone? Ed was right, you can only do your own work. How to incite others is a course I never had. Not these who were here before me, that's certain; those who aren't here . . . these things don't touch them. Almost like a war: you're impressed when you get bombed . . .

Key here . . . here.

Click open, open, shut click.

Must turn in keys today.

Good, yes, it is good, but sad somehow that I can read this board for the last time. This little four-by-five piece of cork hell with its notes from below. Like this . . . new assignments here, for students and attendants. What's this? Someone's drawn a line through Gloria's name . . . here, here . . . wherever it appears. Can only mean one thing: she quit. Or was fired. No, couldn't be fired . . . they need her here. Unless they've got an open order for good squads. She must have quit. Didn't have a chance to see her. Little difference, I guess. We can compare notes on the subway if I ever see her.

Look around. Nothing to look at. Would I stick my mother in here, my aunt, my husband? Depending on how bad, of course, . . . but no turning back, an awful gamble. In a way, no gamble at all, because no one treated as an individual. That I can wager . . . so long as help is incompetent, all-fools'-day every day.

Key here again.

Click open, open, shut click.

This dayroom again . . . this nightmare, this little world, this earth, or something like that. I could walk out of here and come back, say, anytime, say fifty years later, I suppose, like walking out of a dull movie to get a drink of water . . . to go back and find I had missed very little. All the same . . . the same stench—there's a study for someone, the chemistry of stench—these same wretches, the same filth. There's our tatting girlfriend, a perpetual motion machine, could hook her up to a pump, or something, keep the lights working . . .

. . . and my poor naked old experimental lady, naked again. Last act, get another gown . . . why aren't there any attendants in here?

Key.

Click open, open, shut click.

Let's see . . . how the linen stores are. Yes, still plenty here, not torn . . . plenty because hardly ever used . . .

. . . go back with this one. What's that noise upstairs? Sounds like someone throwing a chair against the wall . . . no, too soft. And what's that smell, that smell? As if I didn't know! God, smoke smell. No, not here. Run up, run up the stairs. Oh, don't have to. What? Here comes Nancy and, and Phoebe. What are they doing? Throwing a mattress down the stairs, a smoldering mattress. Phoebe carrying fire extinguisher.

Mattress, plop, plop down the . . . stairs. Smoke puffing out, each plop. Out of breath mattress . . .

"Nancy! A fire? How did it start?"

"How does any fire start?"

114

"That's my line, kiddo, remember?"

"Here . . . help drag this out of doors before the place burns down. No, go upstairs and open the windows, the dorm is full of smoke."

"Okay." I get it, Benson is in pheno . . . before she gets back. She'll skin everybody alive, including her buddies this time. Two steps at a time . . . ooh, what's that? Ugh, a rat, yes, a rat, ran down. I'm running up, a rat's running down. Smarter than I am. These stairs won't last another year. If we could get the women out, we ought to burn the joint down. Top of the stairs . . . dorm. My God, I can hardly see in here! Now we've got smoke on top of stench. Lord, what a mess . . . Phoebe having a ball with that chemical extinguisher, sopping wet floor. Slosh over these wet mattresses, windows, windows. Agnes'll spot this all right. Take a week to dry out . . . cover a dead elephant with a throw rug, no one will notice, not for a second or two. Windows.

I *can't* get these windows open! Not open since 1915, that's why. So why now? Got to get one open, one at least. Well, hell, break it, Seward. Use your eight-and-a half size. There, smash away! What's one broken window in a century . . . except, except it'll be fixed next century. Smoke starting out . . .

. . . that's a little better. At least not so blue in here. Eyes watering, something to cry over all right.

Better see how they're doing downstairs now. Creaky rickety. Well, . . . well, for God's sake! No one here. Tomb again . . . so they disappear back into the woodwork to go on with their miserable little duties of just standing around. Last day like the first . . . tomorrow like yesterday. Used to tear my life off my desk calendar a day at a time. But here . . . clocks should be in years. Where's that gown I left here? Mattress is probably outside, anyway.

115

Let me get my breath. Breath. Gown, gown. Here. No, get another one . . .

. . . one choice certainly. I can look back on my life and say that the little signs of moral breakdown were too subtle for anyone to notice. How was I to know? How would anyone? But it wouldn't be so, for in one little sweat hole of humanity, the breakdown of outlook was complete. Noticing it was inescapable. Yes, I saw it, and I see it, and I let it go. But no one can be in every little sweat hole at once . . . and if we're in sight of one . . . in an awful moment, in a single, terrible moment, I think . . . if we're in sight of one, can we settle for an answer that it was too big, that there was nothing to be done? No, I cannot. I cannot. I cannot let it go . . .

. . . this one, yes, this one, will be all right. Go back with this one. Back to my experimental old lady. Old naked lady. If the world is no better when I leave it . . . than what I found, I can only share the blame if I do not try. Yes, this one will do . . .

. . . can I make such a terrible decision? There just can't be all darkness.

Key.

Click open, open, shut click.

Where is she . . . there, by the window, again, trying to get pneumonia as usual. Sees me. Doesn't turn away. That's a step. Oh, there you are, Phoebe. Back in your chair, arms on arms. Well, the sphinx stinks, I know it, and you know I know it . . . you'll be the same way everywhere you go. Doing as little as you can for the most you can. But it won't bother you, honey, because you'll have a lot of company. Half the world. Just don't do anything . . . don't sweep the floor with pride, don't hammer a nail, write a report, wash a window, put on a bandaid with pride. It's all so much a part of your world. After all, why should you? There, I can ask the question before you do.

Come on, old lady, I have another dress for you. Comes toward me, puts her arms out, and, and feeble, empty smile.

"There you are . . . now, isn't this nice? That's it, turn around." Tie it tightly. Let's see how long you keep this one on. If an hour, we've made another step.

There's the Fleming girl . . . or what's left of her. Been here only a few days longer than I have and completely downhill. Beginning to look like the rest . . . that anonymous ashen decay of humanity. Living, or half-living, proof of my homemade theory that no one will buy: if she can go downhill this fast because of her surroundings, she can be saved by something better. Her one little mistake that she couldn't help . . . now relegated to this, like it was her fault.

And I, who know nothing, would have tried to treat her like an individual . . . and if I failed, she'd not be worse than she is. And for it all, I'd be wrong.

But I'm not wrong, don't dare what the whole world says, to work hard even if the rest are loafing . . .

. . . hardest decision . . . devote yourself to a job you believe in and you know is hopeless. Well, not really hopeless if you believe, but tremendous courage needed. Do I possess it? Just to convince yourself that what you do in your own lonely corner of life will make a, a footpath in a jungle of misery . . . before everything is grown over again. A little cut, a nick, a scratch, where there are no hopes at heart?

. . . should go downstairs. Goodbye old lady. But do I want to say goodbye?

Key again. Here.

Click open, open, shut click.

Oh, oh, Fenwick just put up more notes from the underground. What's she got to say this time? Back to cork hell. I see, new patients coming in and . . . more policy . . .

assignment changes. So official, it even reads clean. I'm supposed to go in and turn in my keys. Feel like slipping them under the door. Otherwise, awkward silence that I can't stand anymore than she can. No, that's not true . . . and I won't do it that way. She must know . . .

. . . what's that noise? Oh, here we go again! That same heart-constricting sound, but it doesn't frighten me anymore. Another chronic, I suppose. Yes, Yes. One big ugly conditioned response . . . field day for Pavlov . . . dayroom door flies open! Phoebe fighting with . . . with, my God, that same woman. Here comes Nancy, out of her part of the woodwork, too. And, and Benson up from pheno! Just ask them, yes, ask them why that poor wretch is still alive. I'll tell you why. We need her for dragging, that's why . . .

. . . everybody yelling, screaming. Benson slips into her act. I knew it. I know it now.

"Oh, come on, Phoebe, goddamn it, kick her down there!" She runs to open hydro door.

No, I won't move, not a muscle. But I'll move later. They've got all the muscle they need. And Fenwick never puts in an appearance.

She'll be dragged a thousand miles before they drag the life out of her. Nose bleeding, this time . . . dribbly path all the way home. Door to hydro slams shut . . . muffled chaos.

No, I cannot let it go. I cannot. The world is filled with fools, and we're all unforgivable . . . and I am just one more fool, maybe in a different way. And maybe I'm unforgivable, too, but it's my life. Fenwick's door not ajar, closed this time . . . no matter.

Go in anyway. Don't knock. Oops, nearly knocked her over. Now what was she doing with her ear to the door?

Surprised to see me? Yes, I'll bet you are. Yes, I know,

who in hell do I think I am bursting in here this way? Well, you've been found out . . . ear to a closed door . . .

She immediately goes to her desk and behind it, gathering herself together. For what? No fight from me, sweetheart.

"So you're leaving us, Miss Seward?"

Don't say a word, Seward, just nod your head . . . slowly, That's it . . . and her face falls in her lap. Nod your head, and . . . and, that's it, just put the keys on her desk.

"I am just turning in my keys, Miss Fenwick."

Aren't you going to say something? No? I thought not. Just pick up your face, old girl . . . I am going to make it miserable for you, old dear, if you care to be around.

Just walk away.

No key this time.

No click open, but open, no click, but shut.

Not an incident, but a course of action . . . important in all our lives. But every course of action begins with one particular second, a minute, an incident. And with that incident begins a wasted life or something you can believe in. If the world doesn't understand, then the world's the loser. But you have to believe it. So you get to the incident . . .

. . . you're a fool, Seward, a fool, a fool! But be a big fool, Seward, a big one.

Epilogue

This is a truthful story. To say it is an attempt to indict the medical profession would be to settle for an easy and abstract explanation; it would be an unjust simplicity. More than that, it would be outrageous. When more than that, it would be untrue.

But this is only the beginning.